I0770751

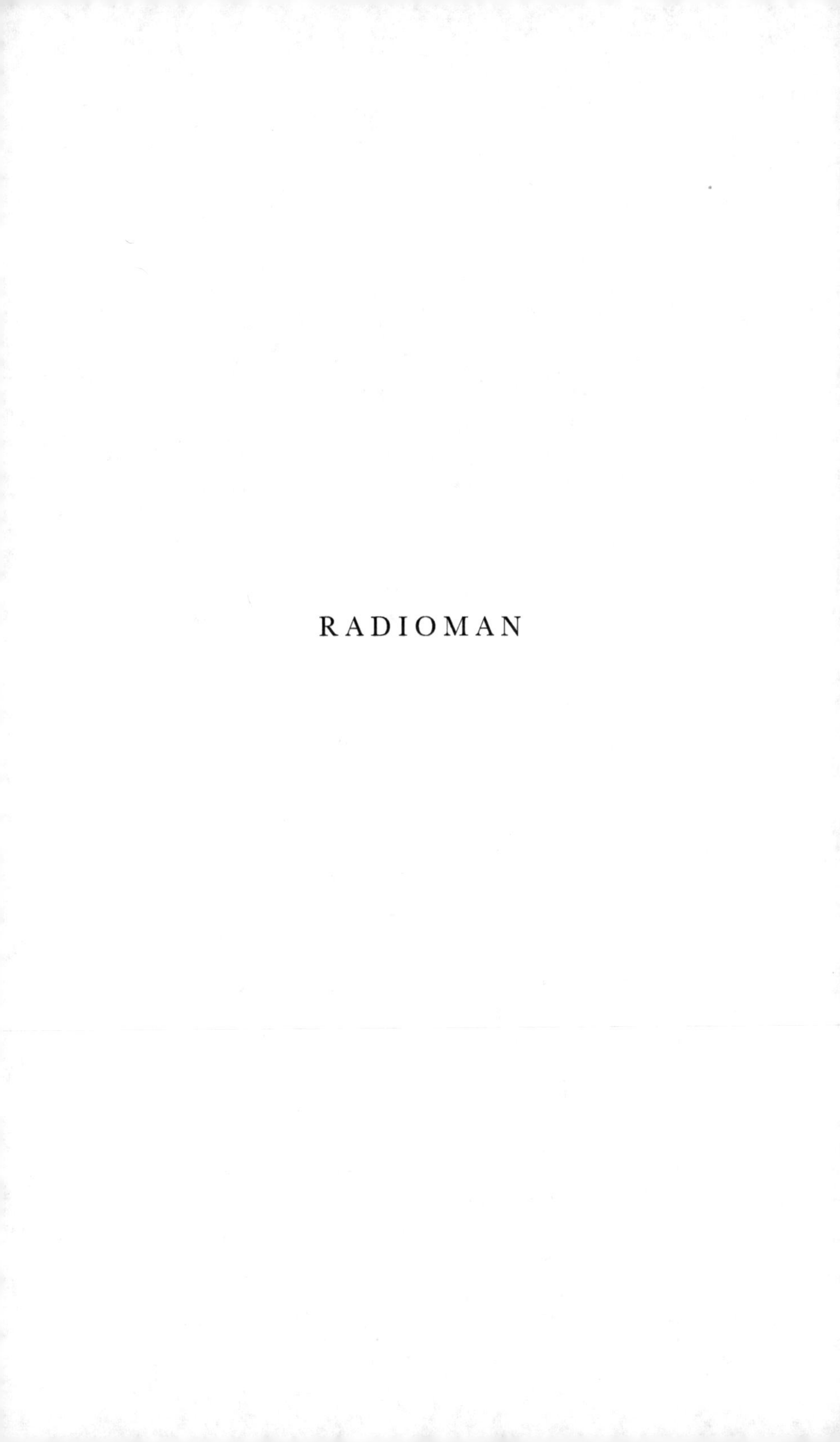

RADIOMAN

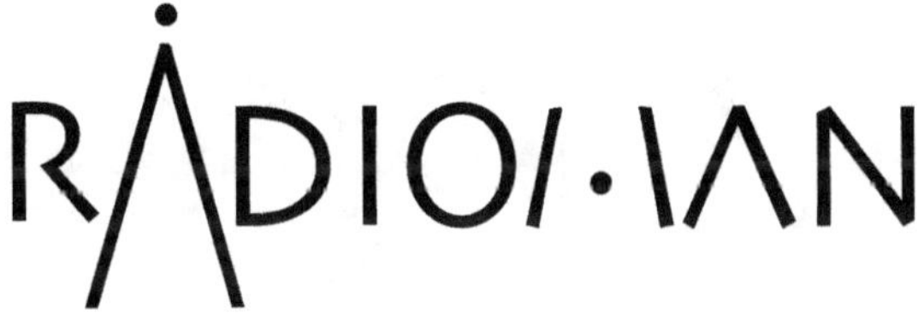

by
Rodney Nakamura

Published by Momo Manuscripts
A Division of El Cheapo Productions

ISBN: 979-8-9893262-1-1

Contents

Summer P.1

Fall P.43

Winter P.93

Spring P.157

Additional P.195

    Maps P.196
    Glossary P.198
    Ranks P.204
    Ribbons P.206
    Wakemaker Segments P.207

Summer

The crackle of dry brush underfoot synchronized with the panicked breathing of an exhausted man. The sound of desperation grew louder and deeper.

Through the rustling of thick grass, the hollow pop of a mortar echoed like a bottle being corked, sending a small grenade-shaped explosive floating upward a meter high. The little canister spun like a top and began to whistle into a high-pitched shrill that pierced the air and climaxed in a mighty explosion.

The pitter-patter of falling shrapnel trickled to the ground. Through the cloud of smoke, a man lay dying. The snuff had done its job.

The Radioman awoke in a dark room. The acrid stench of mildew mixed with the loathsome smell of burnt flesh that lingered heavily throughout the cold and humid chamber. He opened his eyes. A white light beamed from an overhead lamp positioned above his face. Trying to release the tension in his outstretched arms, he felt them anchored down firmly at the wrists: He was being restrained.

From out of the void, a hunchbacked figure approached. The man – if it was a man – hobbled closer, dragging his feet along the damp floor. He was wearing a dingy and ruffled laboratory coat with one sleeve torn at the shoulder, revealing an enormously muscular arm. From the fringe of the light's glow, the Radioman could just make out the outline of a face. It was large and wrinkled with a goblin-shaped nose and blotchy baldhead. The doctor - as he appeared - methodically inspected a series of instruments in preparation for an examination.

"Who are you?" the Radioman asked. "And where am I?"

"Yes, where are you?" the doctor replied.

A needle pierced his arm and gradually the darkness gave way to light. The Radioman felt his consciousness being lifted, transported to another place and time.

Sitting on top of a pile of rubble located inside the ruins of an old cathedral, the Radioman watched as beams of late afternoon sun broke through the crumbling ceiling and cast a blaze of amber hue across the floor.

He looked down and noticed an old photograph in his hand. It was a picture of a rolling hillside with a large oak tree standing alone amongst a sea of grass. The Radioman stared at the image intensely. He knew this place; he had been there before. "Home," he vaguely recalled.

The Radioman continued to concentrate on the picture until his thoughts penetrated through the veil of lost memories. Around him the mason walls slowly dissolved away, and the picture brightened in depth and color until it eventually came to life.

A gentle wisp of fresh air tickled his nose and he felt the tips of dry grass brush against his legs. A sense of serenity warmed his heart and he smiled, for he was indeed home.

In the distance, the Radioman spotted two figures trekking across the hills. Instinctually, he reached above his brow and flipped down a special telescopic lens that was attached to a set of work spectacles. Sharpening the image into focus, the Radioman saw something extraordinary, something that could not be explained but which piqued his interest. What he saw was a large feathery beast with a hawkish beak and furry legs lumbering uphill, while close behind a small ghost-like apparition glided gently in tow.

"What do you see?" The Doc's voice echoed in his mind.

"I see a Griffin and a Ghost," the Radioman replied.

As he watched the two spirits disappear from view, he could hear the faint laughter of children rising. He shifted his attention and spotted a group of youngsters playing under the canopy of a large oak tree.

"I don't believe it… It can't be…" the Radioman wept. "How can it be?"

"You see something from your past?"

"Yes," he said excitedly. "I can see Jumbo playing under Old Gurdy. I can see my sister… I can see myself."

From over the horizon, the jingle of clanking spanners preceded the arrival of a soldier wearing a thick tool belt and shouldering a large radio on his back.

The young girl spotted the dusty repairman approaching from down the hill and shouted with delight, "Papa!"

She ran to greet her father, Alden Harker, and crashed into his legs.

"Hi there, Sneak," he smiled.

As the two snuggled in a warm embrace, the buzz of spinning propellers echoed through the hills. The sound grew louder and deeper until a squadron of pod-shaped fighters swooped in from over a distant peak and thunderously passed overhead.

The oldest of the three children, Jumbo, shouted with great enthusiasm, "They're back!"

The tightly knit formation swept along the contours of the slope and onward toward an airfield located near the coast.

Kiki jumped up with elation, while her older brother, Parker, watched cautiously as a red flare shot upward into the sky.

"Look!" Parker pointed.

Jumbo ran to the base of Old Gurdy and sorted through a pile of gear. He pulled out a pair of hoppers – pressurized pneumatic stilts – and strapped them onto the soles of his boots. Standing up from the ground, the boy bounced in place a few times to equalize pressure within the system. A small valve hissed as the hoppers calibrated themselves and settled into balance.

"I'll catch you guys later," Jumbo waved before trotting down the hill.

Kiki let go of her father and followed in hot pursuit. "Wait, Jumbo! Don't leave yet! I want to go!"

She rushed over to gather her gear and fidgeted anxiously to strap her hoppers onto her boots.

Alden watched in amusement as Kiki wobbled like a drunken ostrich trying to steady itself. Calmly, he walked over and gave her a hand.

"Thanks, Pop." Kiki smiled.

Alden held her hand tightly as she turned to leave.

"And just where do you think you're going?"

"Well," Kiki tried to explain. "I..."

Seeing that she had little time to waste, Kiki quickly manufactured the most innocent expression her little face could muster. Trying to soften up her father with pouting lips and fluttering doe-like eyes, the strange facial contortions ended up looking more painful than earnest.

"I was just, you know, going to help Jumbo?"

"Help him?" Alden raised an eyebrow. "I think Jumbo can take care of himself."

"Sure he can, but… It's like they're always telling us in school: One should never venture off alone, in case something terrible happens. It's always good to have a witness? Or was it an accomplice? I don't know, something like that."

"Is that what they teach you?"

"Sure it is." Kiki looked confused. "Isn't it?"

"Look, Sneak. It's getting late. Besides, I thought you wanted to go home and make motley with me."

"I do. I mean, I did… Yes, I do, but… You know how it is… Please?" she begged. "I've never seen a wakemaker up close before and Jumbo's the only person I know who can get me on the field."

"There'll be other times."

"Not like this. It's a chance of a lifetime and you wouldn't want to deprive me of that now, would you?

Alden listened patiently.

"I promise, only a few minutes. I won't get in the way or cause any trouble. And I won't look at anything secret or scary that might give me nightmares. Please! This could be the most important event in my entire life."

"Oh brother," Parker mumbled under his breath, as he listened to his sister's melodramatics.

"Please, can I go? I'll do extra chores. I'll shovel the muck. I'll study extra hard. Anything."

Alden finally gave in to his daughter's pathetic pleading. "All right, just this once."

"Thanks, Pop! You're the best!"

She sprung up and gave him a kiss on the cheek before scampering off after Jumbo.

"But I want you home by sundown!" Alden insisted.

"Okay!" Kiki waved and shouted. "Jumbo! Hold on! Wait for me!"

Alden looked over at Parker and said, "There goes trouble."

"You said it," Parker agreed.

"Yep, that little beastie's going to be the end of me someday," he sighed. "Well, Park, if Kiki's not coming home for a while, maybe the two of us can have a little fun too. Come on, I'll race you down to the pass… Are you ready?"

Parker quickly threw his pack and hoppers over his shoulder and began running down the hill before his father could say, "Go!"

In the valley below rested the quiet haven of Kakydurn. Kakkie, as it was commonly known, was just one of a hundred or so small communities sprinkled along the east coast of the country of Leialil. Near the town's harbor, an empty field of freshly mowed grass served as a temporary intercept point for Air Armory while a new airbase was being constructed along the Ceelie Launch.

Along the dusty trail, Jumbo stumbled on a loose patch of dirt and skidded to a stop. Sliding in close behind, Kiki crashed headlong into Jumbo's hoppers. Out of breath, she heaved to regain her wind as Jumbo bent down to lend her a hand. She had always seen Jumbo as her protector and inspiration, and like a playful puppy, followed him wherever he went.

"Thanks," Kiki smiled as Jumbo helped her dust off.

Doing a brief check on her hoppers, Jumbo made a few quick adjustments before skipping over to greet the pilots.

At the far end of the field, the last of the porpoise-nosed fighters hovered in for a landing. Jumbo and Kiki watched in awe as the gleaming silver-colored wakemaker came to a gentle rest. A blast of compressed air from one of the turbines blew Kiki backward onto her bottom. Jumbo laughed in amusement as she squirmed to get up. Another blast, this time of steam, depressurized out the engine's exhaust port. Through the foggy mist Jumbo spotted his father, Squadron Leader Hefty Lien, standing tall, rugged, and majestic.

"Hey Pop, get any bites?"

"Not today, Punchy. Sometimes you get the carrot but today we got the stick."

Nearby, Kiki struggled to unsnap the hoppers from her boots. Eager to get a closer look, she opted to unlace her shoes instead and simply go barefoot. Standing little more than a meter high, Kiki gazed up at the huge pod resting directly in front of her. Drawn in by the aircraft's powerful aura, she was instantly captivated and stared in reverence of its grandeur. She had never seen anything so bold and beautiful in her life. The ship's allure beckoned her to reach out and touch it, and unbeknownst to herself, she began to run her fingers along the underside of the wakemaker's fuselage.

From the corner of his eye, the weary pilot caught sight of the child and snapped, "Hey, you! Get away from there!"

Startled, Kiki lurched back.

"I didn't mean any harm," she shivered.

Hefty turned to his son. "You know this kid?"

"Sure. That's Parker's sister."

The pilot loomed over Kiki with a look of inquisition.

"What's your name?" the squadron leader asked gruffly.

"Kiki, sir. Kiki Harker."

"Well, Miss Harker. Look with your eyes and not with your hands."

"I'm sorry," Kiki apologized. "I just couldn't help myself. It's just that I've never had the chance to see a wake close up before."

"Oh, is that a fact?"

"Yes, sir. It's a fact," Kiki's voice trembled.

Realizing he had frightened the child, Hefty softened his tone. "Well, in that case… I suppose if you're gonna do it, you might as well do it right."

The gentle giant removed his flight cap and slapped it onto Kiki's head. The oversized hat draped over her eyes as she was hoisted up onto the portside stabilizer.

"Hop on in there, little lady," Hefty said pointing at the cockpit.

Kiki adjusted the brim of the cap and quickly climbed aboard. She stared in disbelief at the countless buttons, levers, and gauges surrounding her.

"But don't forget," he repeated. "Eyes, no hands. Got it?"

"Right," Kiki replied obliviously.

But like any kid in a candy store, Kiki's curiosity got the better of her. She instantly indulged herself in the many flights of fancy that she would experience as a future ace fighter pilot. Without giving it a second thought, she quickly showed that rules were made to be broken, as she began running her hands over every knob, latch, and switch she could get her greedy little fingers on.

Regretting his decision, Hefty did his best to reign in the unbridled child, but his attention shifted when he heard Jumbo's voice call out, "Pop. Hey, Pop?"

"What is it, Jumbo?"

"Well, like I was saying before, I got worried something bad happened when I saw the flare."

"Hey, it's going to take more than a few pot shots from some Crinch flicker to get me pushing up daisies."

From the other end of the field, a young blind girl named Tilly walked over with the aid of her canine companion Smilie. The boisterous guide dog appeared to recognize Jumbo and his father as he lunged excitedly and scampered over to greet them.

"Whoa, hold on, Smilie!" Tilly said pulling on the harness.

Smilie immediately began sniffing the squadron leader's flight suit and weaving through his legs.

"Easy there, fella," Hefty deflected. "What's going on here? This is supposed to be a secure military installation, not a damn petting zoo. Shouldn't you all be in school?"

"It's summer, Pop," Jumbo explained.

"Excuse me, sir," Tilly interrupted. "But I was wondering if you could tell me where I might find my uncle, Captain Picket. I was told he would be leading B-flight today."

Hefty had made it a policy not to get involved with the lives of his pilots outside of their flight duties, but he had met this girl before and Picket was one of the few he considered a friend. Gathering his thoughts, he steadied himself to deliver the bad news.

"Tilly, isn't it?"

"Yes."

"Pickle," he said clearing his throat, "I mean Picket, ran into a bit of bad luck today."

Tilly was stunned by the news, though she wasn't completely surprised.

"It was real hairy over there," he continued. "Our patrol got caught with the sun in our faces and B-flight took the brunt of an ambush. It was a real muck. And unfortunately, we lost him."

Sensing the gravity of their conversation, Kiki stopped fidgeting in the cockpit.

"I understand," Tilly said solemnly. She shuddered briefly but managed to maintain her composure, "I suppose these things happen. I'm sure you must be used to it."

"No, not really."

"I appreciate your candor, Squadron Leader. And I'm glad you were able to make it back. Maybe tomorrow you can give the Ruddy a message from me and return the favor."

Amazed at the level of grace and dignity the young girl displayed, Hefty replied kindly, "I'll be sure to give them your regards."

"I just hope my uncle didn't lose his life in vain."

"No, he was a fine pilot..."

Squadron Leader Lien struggled to find something more complimentary to say, something that might provide a bit of consolation, but the only phrase that came to mind was the familiar adage, "And a good man."

"Yes, a good man," Tilly repeated sadly.

With a heavy heart, she tugged lightly on the dog's harness and turned away. "Come on, Smilie. Let's go home."

The three watched as Tilly and her canine companion slowly exited the airfield – blinded in battle and touched once again by the cruelty of war.

At the base of the foothills, Parker and his father approached a small glen in an area known as the "Slipper's Pass." They made their way to a stream that meandered through the center of the woods. The water level was low during the summer months, exposing the tops of some of the larger boulders. Soft mud and moss lined the edge of the creek and revealed just how the area had gotten its name.

The dipping sun flickered beams of light through the thick canopy of leaves. Alden took a seat along the water's edge and began to remove his shirt and boots. Parker followed suit but hesitated after touching the water with his hand.

"What's wrong?" Alden asked.

Parker shook his head. "Nothing."

"Well, we better get to it. It's going to get cold once the sun goes down."

"I know, but..." Parker sighed, "It's gonna be a lot colder once I'm in the water."

"Oh," Alden remarked. "How do you know you'll be the one getting wet?"

"Because I always get wet," Parker said flippantly. "Because you're bigger than me and besides, I never win."

"Is that important to you? Winning?"

"Well, it's a heck of a lot better than losing. And it sure beats being cold."

Alden placed his shirt and shoes in a neatly folded packet along the bank and explained, "Winning is nice. It's warm and comforting. But it's only an illusion, Parker. Sometimes we need to get wet in order to know what it is to be dry. You see, winning only means something when the cause is just and true, when it's done out of responsibility and not for pride."

"What's that supposed to mean?" Parker asked. "Are you saying that it's better to lose?"

"No, but it's important to understand what it is you are trying to achieve."

Alden swiped a finger of soft mud and stroked a line across his cheeks and nose.

"But how will I know if something's worth fighting for?"

"In time, when you've lost enough and can see the nature of conflict, you'll know."

Alden rinsed his hand in the clear reflective water and rose from the ground.

Skipping across the rocks, the two positioned themselves at the center of the stream. Alden closed his eyes and listened attentively to the sounds of nature. He could hear the piercing chirps of blackbirds calling through the meadow, the humming of bumblebees busy at work near the shore, and the gentle trickle of water flowing around his peaceful perch.

Parker, on the other hand, stood nervously with his fists clenched in preparation for the bout. He watched with anticipation as his father slowly opened his eyes and nodded back at him. The match had begun.

The two stood poised for battle. Time passed, but neither of them made a move. Parker's eyes twitched and his attention heightened with every movement and sound. After a while, Parker's legs became stiff and his breaths shallow and quick. He scanned his father anxiously for any sign of opportunity that could give him an advantage. But Alden just stood there, solid and still, like an immovable object. Parker knew if he took the offensive, he would be vulnerable to a counterattack, yet he also knew that the light was dimming and the temperature was dropping quickly.

Impatient and growing ever more frustrated, Parker launched headfirst, showering his father with a flurry of punches and kicks. Alden swiftly dodged the barrage, bending, twisting, and leaping from rock to rock. As the match continued, Parker could feel his heart pounding; his muscles were getting tired and his limbs were beginning to feel heavy. He took a brief moment to catch his breath and analyze the situation. He had tried punching high and low, sweeping at his father's feet, and kicking high to his head. "What more can I do?" Parker thought.

A light breeze blew through the foliage. At first it felt refreshing, cooling the perspiration on Parker's body. But as the sun edged below the treetops, the temperature suddenly dropped.

Parker initiated another attack, this time kicking as hard as he could.

Surprised by Parker's ferocity, Alden raised his arms just in time for a block. The force of the impact sent him stumbling back toward the rushing water. He arched his body into a backflip and landed squatting one-footed atop a pointed stone with an exposed crest that was no larger than a fist. Alden could feel the current passing underneath, shifting unstably from side to side. He balanced himself delicately and waited for Parker's next move.

Parker was surprised to see the predicament he had placed his father in, though it pleased him. His confidence began to grow and his mind instantly flooded with delusions of grandeur. "I've got him!" he told himself, "There's nowhere he can go."

A coy grin leaked from the corner of Parker's mouth. "I can do it," he thought. "I can beat him." He inhaled deeply and looked directly into his father's eyes. Convinced of his imminent victory, Parker felt his time had finally come and that the moment he had waited for so long had now arrived - he was going to win!

With a savage roar, Parker lunged forward. He focused on his father's torso and thrust with all his might. A shower of elation rocketed through his body as he shouted with fury. But just as the final blow was to land on its mark, everything suddenly went black.

When he came to, Parker felt a familiar chill rushing over his body. His back was stiff and his vision blurry. A hand reached down to pull him upright. Parker slowly regained his footing and stood up in the shallow water.

"Are you all right?" his father asked.

Dazed, Parker nodded.

"Good."

Parker slowly dredged his way back to the shoreline and took a seat on a nearby log. As he rang the water from his pant legs, he noticed the small stone where his father had been perched resting undisturbed and dry.

"You're getting better," Alden complimented.

Disheartened, Parker huffed. "That's not what the fish tell me."

"Well, everyone's got an opinion."

"I told you, I never win," Parker pouted.

Alden wiped the line of mud from his face. "Be patient, Parker. Give it time."

As Parker continued to squeeze the water from his trousers, he asked. "Say, Pop. Why do you always smear that muck across your face? Is it some kind of lucky charm?"

"No, it's just a reminder."

"Of what?"

"Of what I'm trying to protect."

"And what's that? Dirt?"

Alden smiled. "In a way, I guess. It's a lot of things. This creek, these trees, the hills, this place, this time… You."

Parker looked puzzled. "So you're telling me that we fight so you can protect me? I don't get it."

"Oh, we're not fighting, Parker. We're just playing. You see, when you fight, when you really fight, something in your heart dies and you destroy some part of the world. Do you understand?"

Parker pondered uneasily. "I'm not sure. I think so. But I hope I never have to fight like that."

"Me, too. I hate fighting. But these are difficult times and the Crinch are a difficult lot. They don't believe in logic or reason. Their only goal is to take anything that gives them pleasure. They are blinded by lust and ignorant of their own greed. And what they fail to realize is that without balance, they too will fall."

A strange foreboding resonated in Parker's mind and he asked, "Do you think they're going to win the war?"

"Well, they're on a winning streak. They have the power and the will. But it's a long race. Anything can happen."

Alden finished lacing his boots and hoisted the heavy radio-pack back over his shoulders. "By the way, when you were out there on the rocks, what were you playing for?"

"I don't know," Parker shrugged. "I just wanted to win."

Without saying a word, Alden simply nodded. He remembered how it felt to be young and full of pride and although he knew Parker hated to lose, he also knew that his son had a kind heart and gentle spirit.

Emerging from the gully, Parker spotted a large sonar tower being constructed along an adjacent hill. Excited, he pulled on his father's sleeve and pointed.

"Look, Pop! They're putting up a new birdhouse."

"Yep, they certainly are sprouting up like weeds," Alden sighed. "It's supposed to be online in a couple of weeks."

"Looks like a Gensley mark-two."

"Oh, how can you tell?"

"Well, it has a cone core pickup rather than the old vented slots, but it doesn't have the crosshatch module that's supposed to be included in the mark-three," Parker explained eagerly.

Alden was impressed. "That's pretty sharp. You can see all that from here?"

"Yep. Someday I'm going to be a radioman just like you."

Though flattered by the sentiment, Alden could not help but feel a little sad that his son's dream was so rooted in the mundane technology of war. "That's nice of you to say, but the truth is, I hope someday you won't have to."

"Why? Being a RTO is a great job. The best! I can't think of anything else I'd rather do."

Alden looked at the gleaming white monolith reflecting the rays of the setting sun. "That's funny. Here, I wish I could do anything but this. I remember when I was about your age, in the days before the war. I used to love to sit here amongst the hills for hours, watching the animals graze and the birds soar through the air. I always wanted to be like a bird, unfettered and free. It's been a dream of mine as far back as I can remember. Back then there was no tech, no concrete behemoths pumping out waves of sonic rubbish. Life was simpler, more wondrous, and beautiful."

As Alden reminisced, Parker spotted the silhouettes of Tilly and Smilie standing atop a grassy knoll. Mesmerized, Parker repeated his father's last word, "Beautiful."

Captivated by Tilly since the first day they met, Parker watched longingly as a light breeze fluttered through Tilly's hair and soft linen dress. Unconsciously, he drifted away from his father's side. Guided by the beating of an untamed heart, Parker's mind lofted toward a realm of rapture and romance. Again, his confidence began to brew. Nothing could or would stop him from taking Tilly passionately into his arms, holding her tightly, and dare he think, kiss her. Nothing that is, except the harsh wall of "reality" that struck him when he came to within a few feet of the dazzling young maiden.

Standing face to face with the object of his desires, Parker felt his throat becoming dry and a queasy sensation begin to burble in the pit of his stomach. The illusion that was, was no longer. Unable to utter a simple "Hello," Parker raced to think of something clever to say. He fidgeted silently, bashful, and inept. His heart racing, he struggled to utter a single sound. Luckily for him, the spell of fear was broken when he noticed Tilly wiping tears from her face.

His embarrassment quickly turned to concern and he stuttered, "T-T-Tilly, are you all right?"

Startled, Tilly turned toward the voice and asked. "Parker? Is that you?"

"Yes."

"Parker, what am I going to do?"

"What do you mean? What happened?"

"My uncle… He's dead. What am I going to tell my aunt? What's going to happen to us?"

Parker reached out and touched her arm gently. Tilly responded by gripping him tightly, her hands still shaking from hearing the terrible news.

"I don't know," were the only words Parker could think of. Though he knew she needed something else, something more meaningful and permanent, unfortunately, he had no such wisdom.

"I'm scared, Parker."

Parker wrapped his arms around her and the two stood shivering - one from the brisk evening air blowing against his still damp clothes, the other touched by the hand of death, each finding solace in the other's arms.

It was late when Parker finally arrived home. Alden and Kiki had already finished their dinner and were cleaning the table. Parker stowed his hoppers onto a shelf above the entry. Flames crackled in the fireplace as Alden took a seat in his favorite armchair and began leafing through a pile of schematics.

"Look what the cat dragged in," Kiki shouted from the kitchen.

Alden tapped the bowl of his pipe against a side table.

"Hey, Park! Pop and I made motley, just the way Mom used to," Kiki beamed. "It's delicious. Do you want some?"

Parker said nothing.

Alden sensed something was wrong. At first, he thought it might have to do with Parker's earlier defeat at the Pass, but his instinct told him it was something more serious.

"Everything all right?"

"What's going to happen to her?" Parker asked his father.

"Who?"

"Tilly."

"Well, maybe it would help if I knew what happened."

Kiki released the ladle from her hand as she announced loudly, "Her uncle was one of the pilots that were shot down today."

"I see." Alden ceased lighting his pipe and leaned forward to face his son. "I'm sorry, Parker. I'm not sure what will happen. Death changes a lot of things and it may take some time for her to feel normal again. But you can help."

"How?" Parker asked.

"Just be there. Lend her your ear and try your best to keep her spirits up. In time, everything will work out," he said reassuringly. "You care a lot about her, don't you?

"Yes, very much."

"Parker's in love with her," Kiki waggled exuberantly, batting her eyelids and blowing fish-lip kisses.

Parker darted an evil glance back at his sister.

"It's good to care about others," Alden smiled. "And she's lucky to have a friend like you."

Parker shrugged at the compliment, though deep inside it comforted him to hear it.

"Still, you can only help her so long as you keep yourself healthy. So, what do you say? How about some supper?"

Parker nodded and headed toward the dining table, where Kiki graced him with a heaping bowl of her steaming hot stew.

That night, as Parker and Kiki settled into their respective bunks, Alden entered to say goodnight. Kiki, as usual, squirmed to find an agreeable position, while Parker rested with his hands clasped behind his head and his blanket pulled up to his chin. Alden watched in amusement as Kiki continued to fidget. He waited patiently until she had explored every possible position before finally coming to rest.

"Done?" Alden asked.

"Almost," Kiki signaled. And with a final shake of her head against the pillow, she responded cheerfully, "Done."

Parker rolled his eyes and whispered under his breath, "Nut."

Against the soft chirping of crickets, dull echoes of explosions rumbled from far away. Parker lifted his head and leaned his ear in the direction of the attack.

"Sounds like they're bombing Tenory again."

"Could be," Alden nodded. "But I wouldn't worry. It's a long way from here."

Parker sat up and began counting the number of explosions.

Alden tapped his son on the shoulder. "Come on. It's time for bed."

Parker slipped back under the covers.

Alden leaned over and gave Kiki a kiss on the forehead.

"Night, Sneak," he winked.

"Night, Papa."

He turned to Parker and patted him on the head. "Night, Park."

The sound of explosions gradually ceased.

"Pop?" Parker asked.

"Yeah."

"How long do you think the war is going to last?"

"I wish I knew... But, I wouldn't bother thinking about it much. The Crinch have their hands full fighting over Downy. Who knows? Maybe with a bit of luck, it'll all be over before it's our turn to take the brunt of the load."

"Why do the Crinch hate everyone so much?"

Alden paused before giving an answer. He wondered himself why the people of Criestruden were such an arrogant and angry people, but in the end he surmised it probably didn't matter. The situation was what it was.

"I'm not sure if they hate us," Alden explained. "They're just ignorant, selfish, and a little bit cruel. But in a way they're suffering too."

"Suffering? The Crinch?" Parker asked confused. "That doesn't make sense."

"They're suffering because they have forgotten the natural order of things. Their land is barren but their stomachs are full. They consume in excess but give nothing in return. It's easier now for them to steal what they want rather than repairing the damage they have caused. Bombing, killing, it's the only way left for them to satisfy their hunger."

"But why can't they just leave us alone? What did we ever do to them? Why can't they just fix their own problems? Why do they have to drag everybody else down with them?" Parker became distraught. "Why did they have to kill Mom?"

"I don't know, Parker." Alden answered sadly. "Misery loves company?" He sighed. "Sometimes I think they do it, just because they can. That's the trouble with winning. It often leads to greed."

Upset, Kiki shouted abruptly, "Hey, we forgot Ma's birthday! It was last week."

Alden tried to calm her down, "That's all right, Sneak. It's been a long time. I'm sure she understands."

"No, I should have remembered."

"It's okay to forget things after a while. It's time's way of healing old wounds."

"I still can't believe she's gone," Parker said.

"I miss her," Kiki added.

Alden looked at a picture of his wife sitting along a shelf.

"Don't you miss her, Pop?" Kiki asked.

"Sometimes," Alden replied.

"Only sometimes?"

"I loved your mother, very much. I still do. When I think of her, I try to remember the good times. Love shouldn't hurt. When it does, you're only hurting yourself."

Kiki looked confused. "But I think about her all the time."

"I do too, Sneak. But I've learned to let her go." Alden tried to explain. "You see, sometimes we try too hard to hold on to things. We try to capture some part of them and, in doing so, cause ourselves pain. If you truly love something, you'll learn to let it go. If it loves you, it'll come back."

"But I love Ma. Why doesn't she come back? Doesn't she love me?"

"Of course she does. Maybe the truth is, she never really left. Maybe you just forgot how to find her."

"But you told me she was dead."

"Her body died, but her spirit lives on."

"Where?"

"In you. You and Parker, you're her legacy. You're the memory and the hope of both your mother and myself. Remember that." He turned to Parker. "I watch over you. You watch over Kiki, and so it goes."

"But who watches over you?" Kiki asked.

"Mom," Alden smiled. "She watches over all of us."

"The same way Tilly's parents watch over her?" Parker added.

"Sure."

Kiki snuggled her pillow tightly. "I like that."

"Me, too," Alden said. "The lives of the past are all around us, watching, protecting. If you ever feel lost or sad, look into your heart and listen to the wind. They'll point the way."

Kiki gave an affirming nod.

"All right, you two. It's time to get some sleep."

Alden walked over to the door and turned off the light. "Goodnight."

"Night." The two children answered simultaneously.

Alden exited the room and left a slight crack in the door so a flickering of light could be seen coming from the fireplace around the corner.

"Sweet dreams, Parker." Kiki yawned.

"Night, Sneak." Parker replied.

During the early morning hours, Parker had a dream. He saw a man in a high tower looming eerily and shrouded in darkness. Parker could just make out the outlines of a face – a battle-worn, scarred, and wretched face. He had seen it many times before, as it appeared often in his most frightful of nightmares. Crouched along a railing, like a predator waiting to pounce on its prey, this indomitable image of terror waited patiently for the chance to strike fear upon its victim. Parker knew somehow this premonition, this shadow touched by evil, would inevitably alter his destiny and unleash a horrific tragedy upon him.

A speckle of light flashed in the distance. Parker felt a searing pain brush against his cheek and could taste the saltiness of warm blood as it trickled into the edge of his mouth. He'd been shot!

BANG!!! Parker awoke startled, his face covered in sweat and his pulse racing. A second later, there was another thunderous crash. Parker jumped out of bed and ran to find the source of the commotion. He scanned the living room but saw nothing out of order. It was early in the morning, and his father had already left to work on the radio arrays down by the Hipper Flats. He noticed the entry door pushed slightly ajar, beaming a shaft of sunlight across the wooden floor. From the entry, he could hear the sounds of muffled moans. Quietly, he peeked around the corner and saw Kiki sitting under a broken shelf and rubbing her head.

"What are you doing?" Parker groaned.

"Oh, morning, Park," Kiki greeted him cheerfully. "It's about time you woke up."

Parker's eyes narrowed.

"Say, since you're here, do you think you could give me a hand with my hoppers? Pop put them up too high."

Parker reluctantly retrieved the stilts and handed them to his sister.

"Thanks, buddy."

She dusted herself off and began to attach the hoppers onto the soles of her boots.

Parker leaned in with his arms folded. "And just where do you think you're going?"

"Up to the Chat ruins. I have a message to deliver."

Exhausted by the fright of his earlier nightmare and the raucousness of Kiki's catastrophe, Parker yawned tiredly.

"Look, I don't care what you're planning to do. Just make sure you clean up this mess before you go."

Kiki looked at the clutter strewn across the floor and responded, "But I can't reach that high."

"Well, that's not my problem. Just grab a stool and get to work."

"Can't you just help me? It would be a lot quicker."

"Why should I? It's not my mess."

"Please?"

"No."

Kiki frowned and began to mimic the scolding from her brother.

"Mocking me just wastes time."

Frustrated, Kiki was on the verge of throwing a major tantrum. Luckily for her, just before erupting, she decided to change gears and opted for a different strategy to gain Parker's assistance. In the most pathetic manner possible, she stood up and began to stagger.

"Oh, my head," she moaned. "Wow, that hurts! I hope I didn't suffer a percussion."

"It's concussion, you dingy bat."

"It's ding bat, Parker. I'm a ding bat, not a dingy bat."

"Ding bat, Dingy Bat, Dumb Dumb, Short Circuit, I don't care what you call yourself! All I know is there's a little nut rolling around that cracked shell of yours, and it's rattling like a marble."

He began to chuckle.

Kiki went along with the laughs in an effort to conjure up some goodwill from her brother. Looking up at him with her big innocent eyes, she frowned sadly like a wounded animal in desperate need of help and pleaded, "Parker, could you please help me? I really don't think I can reach up there."

As much as Parker wanted to ignore Kiki's toddler-like tactics, he knew the pestering would never cease and that ultimately he could not win. Knowing that he would always be outclassed by his sister's pathetic pleas, Parker succumbed to Kiki's will and began gathering items off the floor. Satisfied with the results of her dramatic performance, Kiki gave Parker a conciliatory pat on the back and bolstered, "Thanks, brother. You're the best!"

"Don't push it," Parker warned.

While restocking the shelves, Kiki suddenly snapped her fingers and exclaimed, "Ooh, ooh! Hey, I just had an idea! How'd you like to go on an adventure with me today?"

"Ooh! Ooh! No."

"Really, Park! It'll be fun." Kiki encouraged. "I've got it all planned out."

"That's what I'm afraid of." Parker said sarcastically.

"Come on, don't be a wet duck."

"A wet duck? What does that even mean? Look, you do whatever you want. I've got my own plans."

"Like what? Sitting under Old Gurdy, sipping Rilla and daydreaming about your girlfriend?"

"Hey, back off!" Parker snapped. "Didn't I just help you clean up? At least sipping Rilla doesn't get me into trouble."

"It doesn't get you into anything," Kiki smirked. "Please, Parker. You've got to come."

Parker covered his ears and fired back in quick succession, "No, no, no, no, no…"

Kiki grabbed his arm and explained. "But you're the only person I know who remembers how to get there."

"What are you talking about? You've been there lots of times."

"Yeah, but that was ages ago. Those memories are long out to pasture."

Parker rolled his eyes. "Are you for real? It was just last month."

"Like I said, ages," Kiki nodded.

"Besides, what's so important that you'd want to hike all the way up there for anyway?"

"Well, can you keep a secret?"

"Absolutely not."

"Fine, I'll tell you anyway."

She leaned over and whispered into Parker's ear, "I'm going to talk to the wind."

Parker lifted a brow and turned slowly to face his sister. Placing both hands on her shoulders, he stared directly into her eyes and in a calm and sympathetic voice said, "You're crazy."

Kiki scowled. "No, you don't understand. It's not what you think!" She tried to explain. "I'm going to climb up to the top of the ruins. It's got a nice breeze there. And when the time is just right, I'm going to send a message to Mom," she said with conviction. "Just like Pop said. We have to listen to the wind."

"I don't think that's what he meant. That was just a metaphor."

"A what?" Kiki looked baffled.

"A meta–." Parker stopped himself before trying to explain any further. "Just forget it. Look, you can go talk to the wind. You can go climb a rock or jump off a cliff. I don't care. Just leave me out of it. I'm going back to bed."

"Please, Park," Kiki nudged. "Be a sport."

"Goodnight," Parker waved as he began walking back to the bedroom.

Kiki collapsed onto the floor and began to pout. She was an excellent pouter. She held her breath for an entire minute while her face turned red. Secretly, Parker watched from around the corner of the doorway and counted the seconds until his sister would finally give up. After another minute, Parker assumed Kiki must be cheating and turned around to head back down the hallway. However, just as he was about to hop back under the covers, he heard the sound of Kiki's body collapsing onto the floor.

"Aww, jiggers," Parker rushed back and tilted her upright.

Kiki slowly came to.

She asked in a daze, "What happened?"

"You botched yourself, that's what happened," Parker answered. "Holding your breath like a spoiled brat, you actually managed to knock yourself out."

Despite still being in a stupor, Kiki persisted, "So, are you coming with me?"

Parker tapped her on the skull. "Look, brainless. Like I told you before, no. N, O, no."

"Fine." Kiki crossed her arms defiantly. "When Pop finds me lying here dead, you're really gonna get it."

Kiki inhaled and held her breath again.

Teetering on the edge of sanity, Parker clasped his hands behind his neck and began to squeeze his head like a vise.

"Are you insane?" Parker grumbled. "What kind of idiot holds their breath to prove a point?"

A minute passed and Kiki started to turn red again.

Parker threw his head back and clawed his fingers slowly down his face, knowing that he had once again been beaten.

"Okay, enough. Enough! You win!" Parker conceded. "But you'd better keep up, because I'm not waiting for you."

Kiki burst out a powerful exhalation and heaved to catch her breath. "Don't worry about me, old man. I can take care of myself," she smiled smugly.

True to form, it was Parker who was waiting outside to leave an hour later. Kiki, meanwhile, was in the kitchen busily stuffing handfuls of crackers and cookies into her pockets to serve as rations for their trip up to Chatley. Bored, Parker began kicking rocks across the loose gravel track and dragging his boots in a slow pace along the ground.

"Come on, Keek! Let's go!" Parker shouted impatiently.

"I'll be right there!" Kiki's voice echoed back.

From down the trail, the sound of a dog barking was heard. Parker looked up from the ground and spotted Tilly and Smilie approaching. Instantly, his muscles tightened and throat dried as a wave of anxiety washed over him. Combing his hair with his fingers, Parker greeted nervously. "Morning, Tilly."

"Hi, Parker," she replied. "I'm glad I caught you."

"Yeah, we were just getting ready to leave. Kiki and I are heading up to Chatley today. She's got some crackpot idea about talking to the wind."

"Oh…" Tilly nodded politely. "That certainly sounds… Unique. I'm sure she'll find a way to make it memorable."

"Regrettable is more like it," Parker mumbled.

"Who knows? It might be fun."

Tilly's response caught Parker by surprise and he asked timidly, "Say if you're interested, m-m-maybe you'd like to join us?"

"I'm sorry, but I can't."

Parker's heart sank and he felt embarrassed for even mentioning Kiki's lamebrain idea. "Right. Of course, I completely understand." Parker said apologetically. "I know the whole thing sounds pretty ridiculous. Besides, I'm sure you have better things to do."

"No, it's not that."

Parker sensed that something was preoccupying Tilly's thoughts. "Is everything okay?"

Tilly's lips stiffened and she began to weep.

"Parker," Tilly's voice broke. "I'm leaving. I came here to say goodbye."

"Goodbye?"

"Yes. I'm moving to the Meadowlands with my aunt. She has some friends there that we're going to stay with for a while."

"How long?"

"I don't know."

"Do you think you'll ever come back?"

"I hope so."

She leaned in and placed her head on his shoulder. "I'm going to miss you, Parker. You're my best friend," she whispered.

Overwhelmed by sadness, Parker fought hard to keep himself from crying.

"I'm going to miss you too, Tilly."

She ran her fingers across his cheek and gently kissed him.

Parker closed his eyes and felt a rush of energy surge through his body. It was the first time he had ever been kissed romantically. His mind buzzed with ecstasy and his heart raced with exhilaration, but all too soon the moment was over and their lips parted.

"Someday I'm going to cash in on all my bad luck," Tilly declared. "And when I do, watch out." She released her hands and took a step back. "I guess I better get going. I still need to pack a few things before we leave. Take good care of yourself. Give my best to your father and Kiki."

"I will." Parker nodded. "Be safe."

Tilly tugged on Smilie's harness and Parker watched as the two disappeared over the horizon. He wondered what would become of Tilly – the girl of his dreams, his best friend, and first love.

Unaware of what had transpired, Kiki burst out the front door like a rocket, her arms piled high with enough supplies to feed an army. The containers went flying in all directions as she tripped off the front porch and landed at the feet of her brother.

"Ta-da! I'm ready!" she exclaimed boisterously.

Parker stood motionless.

"Hey, what's going on?"

Kiki noticed Parker staring blankly down the trail. She followed his line of vision toward a pair of faint figures disappearing from view. "Who's that?" she asked. "Is that Tilly? Maybe she'd like to join us?"

"She can't… She's going away."

"She's leaving? Where to?"

"The Meadowlands."

Kiki knew by the look on Parker's face that this was serious. Without saying a word, which was tougher than she imagined, she quietly retrieved the scattered boxes and dusted them off.

In a tempered tone, she asked, "Are you okay? Did you change your mind about going to the ruins?"

There was no response.

Kiki nudged her brother. "Parker?"

"Huh?"

"Up to Chat. Do you still want to go? It's okay if you don't. I can probably make it there on my own."

Parker shifted his thoughts back to the present. "No, that's all right. Let's go."

As he began stuffing the food into a satchel, Parker took a last look down the path and wished with all his heart that the future would come swiftly and that someday Tilly would return.

By the time Parker and Kiki reached Chatley, it was well past noon. The sun glowed brightly against the clear blue sky. Thankfully, the slightly higher altitude kept the weather comfortable on this lazy summer day. The thick walls of the outer perimeter showed centuries of wear and erosion. The high timber ceiling had collapsed decades earlier due to the harsh elements and was resting in a mound of sticks and rubble that lined the floor of the now open-air pavilion. Added to that, the more recent bombing raids dotted craters across the landscape and reduced the once great cathedral into a desolate heap of strewn rock and mortar.

Despite the long journey, Kiki was full of energy and eager to complete her task.

Under the canopy of a nearby tree, Parker took a drink from a hydro-canister and set his hoppers against the trunk.

"I can't believe you actually made it here without a single rest or complaint." He wiped the sweat from his brow and complimented, "I'm impressed."

The praise, however, went unheard, as Kiki was already making her way to the base of the ruins. Tilting her head up, she marveled at the enormity of the structure.

She whistled, "Jiggers, that sure is high."

"Are you sure you want to do this?"

"What kind of question is that?" she said dismissively. "Of course I'm sure… I think."

Parker hoisted himself up to a mid-level tier and reached down to lend Kiki a hand. Together, they carefully made their way to the top and took a seat across one of the few remaining arches. From there, they could see the village tucked away in the valley below.

"This is perfect," Kiki smiled with satisfaction.

She took a deep breath and nodded.

"Are you ready?"

Parker shrugged.

"Okay, I'll go first. Wish me luck."

She closed her eyes and listened intently for signs of her mother's spirit.

Parker, meanwhile, leaned back onto his elbows to enjoy the soothing flow of an offshore breeze.

After a short time, Kiki began to show signs of frustration. She opened her eyes and scanned the hills with intense scrutiny. Failing to find what she was looking for, she tapped her brother for assistance.

"Hey, Park. I'm not gettin' anything."

"What?"

"I don't hear her."

"Well, of course you don't." Parker replied. "How do you expect to hear anything when you keep shuffling around like that? Just sit still and try to be calm."

Kiki was perplexed. "That doesn't make any sense. How can I be calm at a time like this? I'll miss my opportunity to talk with Ma. Or worse yet, I might fall off the edge. Maybe you didn't notice, but it's a long way down."

"Don't worry. I'm here."

Kiki rolled her eyes, "That's what I'm afraid of."

Parker snapped back. "Look, do you want to do this or not?"

Kiki weighed her options and nodded.

"Okay. Close your eyes."

She followed her brother's instruction.

"Now, what do you hear?"

"Nothing. Just the wind blowing."

"Relax."

"Maybe nobody's home."

"Look, don't try so hard." Parker tried to guide Kiki even though he himself was doubtful about the whole charade.

Eventually, the frown on Kiki's face softened and the tension in her shoulders released.

"That's better. Now, try to picture the surroundings and imagine the time when Mom was still alive. Got it?"

"Uh huh."

"Good. Keep that thought and focus on it. When you're ready, you can think about what you want to say and send your message."

Kiki projected her thoughts and when she felt her delivery was successful, she gave an emphatic nod.

"Done!" She grinned confidently.

As she leaned back to bask in her accomplishment, a foreboding premonition entered her mind. The thought frightened her terribly and she felt a chill in her spine. Her eyes burst open and she shouted, "No!"

Parker snapped to attention just in time to catch sight of his sister slipping from the ledge.

"Parker!" Kiki screamed.

In a flash, he grabbed her flailing body by the scruff of the collar.

Looking downward, Kiki cried, "Don't let me fall!"

Parker struggled to maintain his grip. "Don't worry, Keek! I've got you."

Kiki panicked and clawed desperately at the shear wall when her shirt began to tear.

"Stop squirming!"

"I can't reach it!"

"Please, Kiki! Stop moving, I can't hold onto you!"

"Save me!"

"Don't worry, I won't let you go!

Rip! The stretched fabric gave way and left Parker with only a tiny remnant gripped within his fingers.

Kiki plummeted downward to the ground and landed feet first onto a pile of rubble. The thrust from the impact buckled her ankles and sent her slamming face first into a large rock. A deep gash was cut under her eye and she felt a throbbing pain reverberate through her head and neck.

Slowly sitting upright, Kiki felt dizzy as specks of light danced like fireflies around the periphery of her vision.

Parker rushed down from the top of the wall as fast as he could. When he arrived at the bottom, he noticed the wound on Kiki's face trailing a line of blood down her cheek.

"Kiki! Are you all right?"

Kiki said nothing as she groggily tried to massage the kinks out of her sprained ankle.

"What happened?" Parker asked.

Kiki shook her head as bits of debris dusted from her hair.

"What do you think happened, butterfingers?" Kiki groaned. "You dropped me."

"I didn't drop you. Your collar, it ripped," Parker showed her the strip of cloth still clutched within his palm. "Are you in pain?"

She socked him in the arm with a vicious blow. "What do you think?"

"Ouch," Parker grimaced.

He took the torn piece of fabric and pressed it firmly against Kiki's face.

"Stop, that hurts!" She cringed as Parker moved her hand up to hold the makeshift bandage in place while he checked over the rest of her body.

"I know, but you have to keep pressure on it to stop the bleeding," Parker explained.

Upon finishing his examination, Parker assessed that on the whole, Kiki was still in one piece. "What spooked you up there?"

Kiki's look turned serious. "I saw her, Parker."

"Who?"

"Mom."

Parker shook his head in disbelief. "I think you must have hit the rock harder than I thought."

"I'm not kidding, Parker. Pop was right. She spoke to me."

"Oh yeah? And what exactly did she say?"

"I'm not sure. It wasn't like she was talking. It was more of a feeling, a warning." The lingering omen echoed in Kiki's mind and she pulled her brother close. "I'm afraid something terrible is going to happen."

A gust of wind rustled through the grass as the two siblings looked up at the ruins looming eerily behind them.

Cautiously, Parker gathered his hoppers and snapped in.

"Come on. Let's get out of here. This place gives me the creeps."

The sun was just beginning to wane when they arrived back at the hovel. Their father had returned home earlier and was relaxing against the entry and smoking his familiar pipe. He spotted Parker stumbling down the dirt trail with Kiki hoisted on his back but did not think much of it until he noticed that Kiki had been injured. The bandage patched against Kiki's face was soaked through with blood and she was groaning in pain.

The pipe slipped from Alden's mouth as he ran over to take Kiki into his arms. "What happened?"

Still trying to catch his breath, Parker panted. "We went up to the Chat ruins and climbed to the top when... I'm not sure what happened, but she slipped and hit her face on a rock."

"What were you two doing up there?"

Parker began to stutter. "Sh-sh-she wanted to..."

But before his son could finish, Alden turned to Parker with a fierce look in his eyes. He was livid. Parker had never seen his father so enraged.

"You were supposed to watch out for her! It's your responsibility when I'm not here!" he seethed. "What were you thinking?"

"I, I, I'm sorry, Pop. It wasn't my... I mean, I didn't—"

"I don't want to look at you right now. We'll talk about this later."

"But —"

"Scat!" Alden shouted angrily.

Parker dashed away as fast as his tired legs would carry him. Alden immediately felt remorse for yelling at his son, but with Kiki bloodied and cradled in his arms, he had more important matters to attend to.

Sitting along the bank of the Slipper's Pass, Parker huddled with his knees pressed against his chest. The evening air was cool and Parker's stomach gurgled with pangs of hunger. Still visibly upset, he wiped tears from his eyes.

"It was an accident," Parker whimpered. "I didn't even want to go up there in the first place. What was I supposed to do? I know that bull-nosed blockhead would have gone off alone and probably would have gotten herself killed. It's not my fault she's a moron. It's not fair." He started to weep. "He didn't even listen to me."

From out of the darkness, a hand gently patted him on the shoulder. "Hey there, Park," Alden began. "I think I owe you an apology." He took a seat alongside and wrapped his jacket around his son. "Kiki explained what happened today. I'm sorry. I shouldn't have yelled at you the way I did. It's just that, at that moment, I was frightened."

"You? Scared?"

Alden nodded.

"But you're not scared of anything."

"I wish that were so," Alden grinned. "But the truth is, I'm scared of a lot of things. When I saw Kiki there covered in blood, I was terrified. You and her, you two mean the world to me."

Parker felt relieved to hear those reassuring words. "I'm sorry too," he said. "I should have been more careful."

Parker knew the trust Alden placed in him and he took the responsibility seriously. With firm conviction, he faced his father and made a solemn pledge. "Don't worry, Pop. I won't let it happen again. I promise."

Having never seen his son so resolute before, Alden knew Parker meant what he said. "I know, Parker. You always try to do the right thing. Just make sure it doesn't weigh too heavy on your shoulders and get you down. Besides, Kiki isn't always going to be a kid. She's going to grow up someday and eventually she'll have to learn to take care of herself. Until then, let's try and keep an eye on her and do our best to catch her when she falls." Alden offered his hand. "Deal?"

"Deal," Parker shook.

By the time Parker and Alden reached the outskirts of town, they were joyfully laughing about the day's earlier debacle.

"…And of course," Parker giggled, "not only did she trick me into cleaning up her mess, she also duped me into taking her up to creepy old Chat to have a vision or something. I figure you and mom must have gotten seduced by a charmer. Or better yet, I bet she was raised by a pack of wild animals, and you guys just happened to take her in as a pet. Please tell me that's true."

"I'm afraid not," Alden laughed. "That one's definitely ours. It's the price I pay for being a bit of a handful myself when I was growing up."

"Talking to the wind," Parker mocked. "Give me a break."

Alden paused. "Whoa, hang on there. What's so crazy about that? You don't believe she did?"

Parker shrugged. "Well, you've got to admit that it's a little farfetched."

"Perhaps. But it's a big world, Parker. Anything can happen."

"I don't know, maybe," Parker shrugged. "But I wouldn't bet on it—"

Suddenly, a roar buzzed in from behind the foothills. The noise grew louder and closer until a wave of enemy bombers soared in from above. They looked like huge sea rays with wide sweeping wings and flattened fuselages. As they were passing overhead, Parker and Alden dove to the ground. The thrust from the powerful pulse jet engines spewed trails of caustic black smoke across the twinkling moonlit sky.

When they caught sight of the aircraft again, the bombers had already released their explosive ordnance. The din of detonators whistled briefly before the bombs exploded in quick succession and struck a line of destruction straight through the middle of the village. White-hot flames cast an ethereal corona over the landscape as burning buildings glowed like cinders of coal arranged in a gigantic fire pit. Then, in a moment's flash, the raid was over.

Alden lifted himself from the ground and wiped the dirt from his face. He saw a path of craters dotting a line from the foothills to the town. It was then that he noticed the family hovel where Kiki was resting had been hit.

"Kiki!" Alden screamed.

Terrified, Parker shivered.

"Stay here!" Alden ordered. "Do you understand? Don't move. There might be a second wave coming through. I'll come back to get you as soon as it's safe."

A thousand terrible thoughts rushed through Alden's mind as he neared the crumpled homestead. He could hear the muffled pleas of his daughter echoing from under the debris and he immediately began to shovel dirt with his hands.

"Help! Someone, please help me!" Kiki wailed.

"I'm here, Kiki! Just hang on!" Alden shouted back, looking for signs of his daughter. "Where are you?"

"Papa! I'm stuck! I can't move!"

"Don't worry, Sneak. I'll get you out!"

With almost superhuman strength, Alden lifted huge sections of broken timber until he finally came across one of

Kiki's hands poking out through the rubble. He dug exhaustedly trying to free her trapped torso.

Kiki cried hysterically as the sound of a second wave of bombers rumbled in for an attack.

Alden yanked Kiki's arm as hard as he could. The power of the jolt nearly separated her shoulder and she cried out in pain. Reaching under her armpits, Alden pulled and shouted. "Wiggle, Kiki! Wiggle your legs!"

She strained and contorted her body in every possible direction until she was finally able to set herself free. Alden quickly lifted Kiki in his arms and ran back up the hill.

Detonators shrieked as the bombs began to fall.

Parker covered his head as he watched a massive blast hurl Kiki from their father's arms.

Alden dropped to the ground, his body smoldering from the searing bits of shrapnel embedded in his back.

"Papa!" Kiki shouted.

The two children rushed over and rolled him face up.

Alden's expression was serene and calm. He winked at Kiki and said. "You okay, Sneak?"

"I'm fine, Papa. How are you?"

"I'm a little tired," Alden exhaled.

Kiki began to weep.

"Shh… Don't cry, Sweetie. Everything's going to be all right," he reassured. "Now, promise me you'll do your best to listen to your brother and stay out of trouble, okay?"

"No, Papa," Kiki sobbed, clutching her father's hand. "You need to stay with us."

"I'll always be with you." Alden said, tapping her heart.

Alden turned to Parker and whispered, "I'm sorry, Park. I wish it didn't have to be this way. I know she's a handful, but I have faith in you."

"No, Pop. I can't do it!" Parker wept. "I'm not ready."

Alden clasped the children's hands together. "Look out for each other. Be good."

"No, Pop! Please!" Parker pleaded. Wrought with fear, Parker ran away from the pain, away from death.

"Parker!" Alden gasped. "Come back…" He heaved as his lungs expelled a final exhalation.

Unable to contain her grief, Kiki collapsed on top of her father. "Papa, don't leave me! Papa!" She pounded on his chest in a feeble attempt to revive him. But all her efforts were in vain, for Alden had already passed.

Sprinting up the foothills, Parker tripped over a large rock and stumbled to the ground. His heart racing, he tried to catch his breath as he stared up at the night sky. A tall tower stood erected nearby. The elegant spire reminded him of his father and the days he'd spent waiting to hear the clanging of metal spanners that signaled his return.

He murmured softly. "You can't die, Pop. Who's going to take care of us? I thought we had a deal." Parker clasped his hands and begged the spirits above. "Please, bring him back! I'll do anything." A blanket of clouds drifted overhead and he closed his eyes. "Mom, if you can hear me… Please help. I can't do it alone."

The sound of approaching footsteps broke his concentration and he heard his sister shouting from below.

"Parker! Parker! Where are you?"

Parker wiped the tears from his eyes. "Over here."

Kiki spotted her brother sitting in the tall grass and crashed into his arms. She grabbed him tightly and began to cry.

"Parker! Why did you leave? Pop's dead! He's dead, and I couldn't find you!"

Parker struggled to calm her down. "I'm sorry, Keek," he said guiltily. "I just couldn't stay there."

"What are we going to do, Parker? What's going to happen to us now?"

"I don't know."

In the wake of destruction, the Harker children, now orphaned, huddled together under the moonlit shadow of the sonic array as billows of smoke rose from the village below. Their childhood severed, the innocence and safety they once enjoyed had come to an end and Parker and Kiki were now alone.

Fall

Seven years had passed, and the community of Kakydurn and its gentle landscape had finally healed. Bathed in golden brown, the village once decimated had been restored to its original splendor and again rested as a quiet and peaceful haven. One could only see indications of the passage of time by the multitude of technology that sprinkled about the foothills like dots on a map. There were sonar platforms called Birdhouses and anti-aircraft installations nicknamed Slingers. There were Thumpers, Hedgehogs, Cattails, and Dupes – all connected in a vast network designed to detect and protect against the possibility of an enemy invasion.

Perched high atop one of these massive arrays was a young woman dressed in tan coveralls and layered in a cumbersome utility vest that was littered in a myriad of tools and widgets. The crowning jewel to this already ample ensemble was a bulky radio pack with a long whipping antenna hoisted onto her back. This small-framed girl of eighteen years was Kiki Harker. She was petite and possessed a cute and innocent smile. But anyone who knew her understood that she was definitely a tomboy. Throughout the years, she maintained the same mischievous look in her eyes – a point underscored by the scar she received on that fateful summer day when she and her brother ventured to the Chatley ruins as children.

The weather was warm on this day of equinox, but that soon would change, as autumn was fast approaching. Caught in a tangled web of wires, Kiki busily tinkered with a series of broken electrical connectors from one of the main junction relays. Frustrated, she dropped the cable ends and kicked the access panel with her boot.

A voice shouted from below. "Yeah, kick it harder! That'll show it who's the boss!"

Kiki looked down and spotted her brother staring upward with the same exhausted look of disapproval she had seen a thousand times before. Parker, as a young man, looked very much like his father, though his body could use a year or two more of filling out. Both the Harker children had enlisted in military service upon completing their primary education and like their father before, became radio operators in defense of the country.

A pair of exposed wires jolted Kiki and she threw her calibration wrench angrily at the tower. Ricocheting off the metal superstructure, the delicate instrument tumbled a hundred feet to the ground and landed just inches from her brother's feet.

"Hey, watch it! You almost killed me!" he shouted. "You know that's sensitive stuff you're banging around up there."

"This rusty old fossil? Pile of garbage should have been torn down years ago. Why can't the Crinch ever get a lock on this piece of junk and do us all a favor?"

Parker shook his head disapprovingly at Kiki's surly response. He picked up the metal tuning fork and twirled it between his fingers. "So how much longer are you gonna be? I need some help adjusting the range trajectory on Hedgehog four-one-eight."

"Again? Didn't we just tune that wreck a week ago?"

"Hey, I don't make 'em, I just fix 'em. It's picking up a glitch in one of the jumpers so it needs an acoustic wash."

Kiki ignored Parker and went on searching for the missing tool.

Snapping her fingers, she remembered just where the little instrument had gone. She yelled down to her brother for assistance.

"Hey, I think I dropped my fork. Can you bring it up here?"

Annoyed, Parker exhaled a deep breath before slipping the tool into his vest pocket.

"Hang on."

As Parker prepared to ascend the tower, Kiki impatiently yelled, "Come on, Park! Shake a leg! This box is going to blow by the time you get here."

Parker was tempted to make a smart remark but knew if he was going to get any help at all, he should swallow his pride and take the high road. "All right, keep your pants on!"

He pulled out a small magnetic chuck and snapped it onto a pulley that hoisted him to the top.

High above the ground, the air was cool and refreshing. Parker stepped onto a thin grated ledge and snapped a safety line onto the tower. He walked over to his sister and saw her fumbling about in a mess of cables and connectors. Watching in amusement, Parker clicked a snippet as Kiki struggled to free herself from her entangled web of handiwork. His look, however, suddenly turned grim when he realized just how long it was going to take to repair the damage.

He grabbed a handful of twisted wires and asked, "What's this?"

"Hey, lay back! I'm not finished with it yet," Kiki explained. "It'll turn out. You'll see."

"Here," Parker said, handing her the wrench.

"Thanks," Kiki nodded. "Just put it down next to that breaker."

Parker wanted to point out the obvious error in her judgment and knew if she didn't immediately strap the tool back into her vest, the tarnished little spanner would soon be destined for another fruitless bout with gravity. Still, he decided that discretion remained the better part of valor and placed the wrench on the floor where Kiki instructed.

While checking over the schematics, Kiki looked confused as she struggled to sort out a computation in her head. Giving up, she picked up a pair of cables and tried again to splice two unmatched connectors. There was a loud pop and a shower of sparks. Kiki flinched from the jolt and, just as predicted, kicked the precariously placed spanner back down to the ground below.

"Damn it!" she shouted.

Parker looked at the mess and could not contain his frustration any longer. "Jigs, what the heck were you thinking? You could have blown both of us up kingdom come. Why didn't you shut off that load capacitor before you started tinkering with it? It's basic flow dynamics. Besides, you know the direct current rate's too high for a passive link. You're gonna send flags out over the entire network."

"Well, I couldn't turn it off," Kiki informed.

"Why not?"

"Because..." she paused, licking the tips of her blackened fingers. "I don't have a spigot."

"What do you mean, you don't have a spigot? How can you do any work if... Wait a minute, are you telling me you lost your turnpike again? That's the third one this month."

Kiki ignored him.

"I don't think Aux is going to requisition you a new one, since I'm pretty sure they've already labeled you as a bad investment."

"Well, maybe you can get me one," Kiki grinned. "Just say you lost yours."

"What? No. Why would I want to go on report and get blackballed?"

"Geez, I guess Pop was right. Power does corrupt."

"What are you talking about?"

"You've changed, Parker," Kiki sneered. "Ever since you made specialist, you act like you're my boss or something."

"But I am your boss."

"No, you're just another channel rat like the rest of us," Kiki said indignantly. "And you only got promoted because you're older than me... You know, it's sad. I remember when you used to be one of the bunch."

"Hang on, I am one of the—" Parker caught himself falling again for one of his sister's devious guilt trips. He waved a finger at her, "No, Keek. Not this time. This time you're on your own."

Kiki folded her arms in defiance.

"Unbelievable," Parker mumbled. He took a moment to calm himself down before resuming the conversation, "All right, where do you think you lost it?"

Still upset, Kiki rolled her eyes and tapped Parker on the head. "Hello, brainless. I don't know where. That's why it's lost. Look, don't hassle me!"

Parker picked up the mismatched cable ends and cross-referenced the identification numbers. After reviewing the schematics, he found the corresponding connector and spliced the two together. Dusting off his hands, he turned to Kiki and asked, "So, what's with you today?

"I'm fed up with it," she said curtly.

"It?"

"All of it."

"All of what?"

She pulled at her faded fatigues and utility vest. "This, I hate it!"

"What are you talking about? Your clothes?"

"No! This… This job," Kiki huffed. "Don't you get it? I want to do something with my life."

"You are," Parker said proudly. "You and me, we're the backbone of this entire war."

"Right," she grumbled. "Twistin' dinks and punchin' code ain't my idea of backbone.'

"But it's important," Parker continued. "Without early detection, the Crinch would have–"

"–Bombed us out years ago," Kiki interrupted. "Yeah, I know. I've heard it all before." She wiped the sweat from her brow. "Look, Parker, I know it's important, but it's just not enough. Not for me. I need to dig in. I need to get my hands dirty."

"They are dirty."

"You know what I mean. Maybe it's all right for you to sit around on the back burner, but I want to get in there, on the frontlines making a real difference."

"Oh yeah? And just what would you do?"

As if on cue, a pair of low-flying wakemakers swept over the horizon, skimming the contours of the foothills.

Kiki pointed. "That!"

"What? A pilot?"

"Sure. Why not?"

"No, that's fine. So long as you like having wings nailed to your coffin."

"We're all dying, Parker."

"Don't blow me smoke. You know what I mean," Parker said sternly. "Besides, I wouldn't let you."

Kiki's blood began to boil. She pursed her lips and her nostrils flared. "Wouldn't let me?"

Realizing he might have overstepped his authority, Parker raised his hands in surrender in an attempt to defuse the tension. "Look, Keek. I'm responsible for you. You're the only family I've got and I made a promise to watch out for you."

"And you did," Kiki interjected. "But I'm grown up now."

"You're not that grown up."

"Park, what happened? I used to look up to you. I thought you were strong. I thought, of all people, you'd want revenge."

"Well," Parker paused. "I grew up."

Over the years, the image of their father's death still haunted him and even now sent shivers through his body.

Kiki stared at Parker with a look of contempt. "Fine, but I'm still mad as hell. This war took our parents. Doesn't that make you angry?"

Parker fidgeted uncomfortably. "No, it just makes me sad… And it taught me a very valuable lesson."

"Oh? And what's that?"

"It taught me to be cautious."

Kiki rolled her eyes. "Scared is more like it."

"Call it whatever you like," Parker said defensively. "At least I'm not going to get myself killed chasing after some damn worthless glory!"

"Worthless? This is our home we're talking about!"

"Look, Keek. Fighting isn't going to bring back our parents and outside of that it's just land," Parker refuted. "It's not worth dying for."

"Oh yeah? Well, Pop would have fought for it! And besides, if this land isn't worth fighting for, then what is?"

Parker clenched his teeth as he contemplated his response. He wanted to put Kiki in her place but realized that for him there could be no truthful answer to her question.

From below, a man dressed in heavy infantry gear and shouldering a large pneumatic rifle approached the tower and whistled. From his formidable stature, the once husky-framed boy had transformed himself into a chiseled, muscular hulk, and the once playful nickname that marked him as a child seemed still fitting for this rugged man of war was indeed Jumbo.

He laughed, "You two at it again?"

"What else is new?" Kiki replied.

Jumbo set his rifle on the ground and took a seat at the base of the array. "So did you tell him the good news?"

Kiki signaled Jumbo to be quiet.

"What news?" Parker asked.

"Nothing. It's nothing."

"Come on," Parker pressed. "What's the big deal?"

"I'll tell you later," Kiki deflected.

Parker looked at her suspiciously as she slowly latched the unfinished panel back into place. Seeing that he was not going to get any further explanation, he tried to coax the answer out of Jumbo, "That's great, Jumbo! When did you get the word?"

"Just after lunch!" Jumbo said excitedly. "Can you believe it? We're in! Both of us, we actually made it!"

Parker continued with his false front. "So what's next?"

Kiki stood stiff-lipped with her back turned to her brother.

"Well," Jumbo continued, "Since we both made grade, Air Armory is going to send a transport out to rotate us into OCS."

Shocked by the news, Parker reached out and spun Kiki around to face him. "What is he talking about?"

Kiki tried to explain. "Parker, it's like what we were just discussing. You know, about purpose."

An intense scowl came over Parker's face and he said lividly, "You stupid, stupid idiot! I don't believe this!" His arm shaking, he pointed a finger up to Kiki's face. "Never! Do you hear me? Never!"

Fuming, he collected his tools and prepared to descend.

"Look, Parker. Maybe our parents or this land isn't enough to get you excited, but they mean a lot to me. This is my home, too. And I, for one, am willing to die for it!"

"You're not going anywhere, do you hear me?" Parker snapped his chuck back onto the pulley. "I don't ever want to talk about this again. Do you understand me? This conversation is over."

As he rappelled to the ground, he could hear Kiki yelling down at him. "It's not over, Parker! Not by a long shot!"

Touching down, Parker detached from the tower and picked up his hoppers.

Unaware of the subject of their argument, Jumbo smiled at Parker, "Sounds like someone's pretty hot."

His chin tucked down, Parker pushed past Jumbo grumbling, "This is all your fault."

"My fault?" Jumbo was confused. "What's going on?"

Snapping into his hoppers, Parker leaped away across the dry grass as Kiki voice echoed, "You can't stop me, Parker! It's my choice! Mine!"

Later, as the evening sun set in the distance, Kiki made her way over to the Mounds at Bramble Point. She looked out over the inlet shallows as sparkles of light danced off the surface of the water.

Still seething, she kicked a clod of dirt with her boot and muttered, "Bloody ogre, who does he think he is anyway? All my life, he's been nothing but a nag. It's high time someone took him down a peg." She picked up a small stone and tossed it into the water. "I'll show him. He'll regret the day he tried to tell me what to do."

A message buzzed in on her diagnostic recorder and a series of spools began spelling out a message. Realizing it was from Parker, she spitefully pulled the plug from its socket and tossed the device to the ground.

She turned to face the Ceelie Launch, and dreamed of the adventure waiting for her beyond the horizon. A gentle breeze blew in from the shore and helped to cool her temper. She picked up the dusty keypad from the ground and stowed it back into her utility vest. Filled with purpose and conviction, she snapped on her hoppers and made her way back to the trail.

At the hovel, Parker finished dinner alone. He left a plate out for Kiki and moved to the sitting area where a fire crackled under the mantle. He took a seat in the old armchair his father once enjoyed and glanced at a nearby side table overflowing in a pile of half-repaired circuits, spare parts, and other miscellaneous widgets. Shuffling through the mess, Parker pulled out a broken rheostat and began to fiddle with it.

He heard a pair of boots stomping on the front porch. The door creaked open and Kiki entered. Quietly, she hung her hoppers up in the entry and walked a direct line past Parker straight to her room.

Tossing her utility vest onto the bed, Kiki unbuckled the heavy tool belt from around her waist and let it drop to the floor. The metal instruments clinked as they settled onto the wooden planks. She flopped to the ground and pressed her chin up against her knees. Sitting in silence, she noticed a small object glimmering under the dresser across the room. She crawled over and retrieved the tiny object with her fingers. It was nothing special, just another chrome-plated audio chip that probably contained some useless information – daily notes or a downloaded status report. She raised the metallic token up to her face and blew off a thin layer of dust. Through the reflection, she noticed the pinkish scar lined under her eye that told the story of her childhood mishap. Grabbing the recorder from her utility vest, she placed the chip into a playback slot.

"Hey, Sneak," the voice spoke cheerfully. "If you have a chance, do me a favor and restock the wood for the fireplace. Ask Parker to help if it's too heavy for you to carry. Oh, and don't forget to wear an extra pair of socks today. It's pretty cold out. That reminds me, we have to get you a new pair of boots." Tears welled in her eyes as she listened to the recorded message left by her father. "Have a good day at school. I'll see you tonight," the message fizzled.

There was a knock and Kiki looked up to see Parker standing in the doorway fidgeting with the broken rheostat.

Quickly, she stifled her emotions. "What do you want?" she asked, avoiding eye contact with her brother. "I'm not talking to you."

"I'm sorry about today."

Kiki sat stoically.

"I heard the snip," Parker commented. "It was nice to hear his voice again. It's funny. Sometimes I feel like he's still here."

"But he's not," Kiki said bluntly.

"Keek, I know you feel like I'm interfering with your life. But I can't let you go off and fight. I made a promise. A promise to keep you safe and out of trouble."

"Give me a break," Kiki said dismissively. "Look, Parker. I'm not a little kid anymore. I've made up my mind and there's nothing you can do about it. I'm going."

"Right. I'm sure it's easy for you to pick up and do as you please, but I won't..." Parker paused and rephrased. "I mean, I don't think you should do this."

"I thought you said this conversation was over."

Parker tried his best to calm the situation. "Why didn't you at least tell me what you were planning to do?"

"Because I knew you'd never let me go and we'd just be fighting about this earlier," Kiki sighed. "Besides, I wasn't sure if I'd even qualify."

"Well, of course you'd qualify. We're losing this war, and Air Armory is running out of bodies to send up."

Kiki felt slighted by the comment but said nothing.

Parker leaned his forehead against the doorway. "You know, there's something I never told you about that night, when Pop died... I got a glimpse of something that changed me forever. Something that I didn't want to believe but could not deny."

"Oh yeah? And what's that?"

"Reality, the cold hard truth. That life is brutal and unfair. That heroes and victory are just fantasies, figments sprung up in the imagination of children. The only real salvation in war is to survive."

"You're wrong. It's not enough just to survive. You have to fight for what you believe in. You might not see it, but this place is more than our home. It's the only good thing left in this world. The damn Ruddy have exploited or destroyed just about everything else. They might take our land. They might even win the war, but I swear I'll do everything in my power to stop them. Like the old saying goes, 'sincerity lies in your guts.' And if that's true, then I'm ready to let mine spill."

"What the hell does that mean? Where did you get this stuff? Sincerity lies in your guts?" Parker scoffed. "Who told you that? Jumbo?"

"It doesn't matter, Parker. It's true. You can argue with me all you want, but it doesn't mean a damn thing."

Parker warned, "Kiki, if you leave here, you'll die."

"Yeah? Well, better dead than a coward," Kiki retaliated.

Parker was deeply hurt. Feeling betrayed and insulted, he smashed the rheostat against the doorframe and stormed out of the room.

Kiki quickly realized she had crossed the line and though she knew her words were spoken out of spite, pride kept her from apologizing.

The front door slammed shut and the sounds of Parker's footsteps faded into the distance.

At the top of the foothills, Parker took a seat under Old Gurdy. The cold night air condensed his breath and he whispered to himself, "I'm not a coward. I'm not." The winds rustled the dry grass in a rhythmic tone that sounded like shifting sand. He closed his eyes and tried to calm his mind. "Why do things have to change?" he asked. "Why does everything have to be so complicated? And why is this world so full of cruelty and death?"

He looked up at the stars for guidance. "What am I supposed to do?" he asked the spirits above. "I can't stop her. She's just too stubborn." Parker pulled in his knees and curled into a ball. He felt blood trickling from his palm, cut by the sharp edge of the rheostat. There he sat silently under the canopy of the lone oak tree, pondering a future that was yet unknown.

As the early morning light diffused through the bedroom window, Kiki finished packing her gear and headed out to the airfield. A light fog had settled over the dew-laced grass and squished under her feet as she trekked toward the landing zone. Through the haze, she could see Jumbo standing next to a docked transport waiting for her.

She scanned the hills for signs of her brother. She felt guilty for arguing the night before and hoped she could patch things up or at least say goodbye before leaving.

Jumbo jogged over and took the heavy sack from Kiki's hands. "Morning, Keek," he greeted in his typical chipper fashion. "I guess this is it. We're finally getting out of this grassy wasteland."

"You said it," Kiki responded with a forced grin.

"Where's, Parker? Isn't he going to see us off?"

Kiki shrugged.

"Still mad, huh?"

Jumbo handed the luggage over to a flight conductor, who stowed the rucks into a compartment located on the ship's undercarriage. Without saying a word, the conductor motioned for the two to climb aboard. Kiki took a last lingering look at her home. She wanted to etch that peaceful moment into memory so she would always remember the roots of her convictions.

Jumbo tapped her on the shoulder. "Are you all right?"

She nodded half-heartedly. "Let's get out of here."

The transport's mighty turbines whirred to life and Jumbo and Kiki climbed aboard. Pneumatic compressors began hissing as the aircraft pressurized for departure. The hatch sealed behind Kiki as she took a seat next to Jumbo. Staring out of the side window, her thoughts weighed heavily. She questioned whether it was the right decision to leave. That question, however, had now been rendered moot, for the ship was taking off.

From the field below, the buzz of propellers awoke Parker. He stood up and squinted to make out the transport against the bright glare of the rising sun. He knew instinctively that both his sister and Jumbo were on board. A deep sadness washed over him when he thought of the promise he had failed to keep. From this point forward everything would be different. For the first time in his life, Parker was alone, and not just alone, but left behind. He waved goodbye and wished, "Good luck," as the tiny silhouette of the glistening aircraft slowly disappeared from sight.

* * *

Another summer had come and gone since Kiki left home and once again fall was fast approaching. With the last remnants of summer heat subsiding a few weeks earlier, the current weather was cold and dreary. Along with the shortened daylight hours, dry grass lay dormant on the hills; the trees lining Slipper's Pass had just begun to shed their leaves in preparation for the oncoming winter.

Life for Parker was equally dismal. He had settled into a dull and lonely routine, one that consisted of fixing radio towers by day and practicing the lessons taught by his father at night. Luckily for him, this solitary low came at a time when a prolific new wave of technology was being dispensed throughout the country's defensive network. With Kiki away and old equipment being continually upgraded, Parker had more than his fill of tinkering to attend to.

Despite having submitted the paperwork for a replacement, his request must have gone unnoticed, for he had not heard a single word about any rotations coming through the sector in over six months. With no re-o on the way and his two closest companions off to fight the war, all Parker could do was to keep his route as prepared as possible to defend against the Crinch. He wanted to prove to Kiki and himself that this work he believed in was indeed important.

One afternoon, as he finished aligning the passive collectors on an old birdhouse, he came across a tarnished metal spanner lying on the ground. He picked up the instrument and noticed the name "K. HARKER" engraved on the side. With a melancholy gaze, Parker recalled the argument he had with his sister on that fateful summer day.

"I can't believe it's been a year," Parker reflected as he slipped the wrench into his vest pocket and began making his way down the hill.

The diffused sun projected a soft glow through a layer of billowy clouds that stretched overhead. Tempted by the sight of Old Gurdy swaying gently nearby, Parker decided to take a short break before completing the last assignment of the day – fixing the old Hedgehog that had been on the blink since the day it went online. He took a familiar seat against the base of the tree and flicked open his com-link to give an update on his latest assignment.

"Daisy Point, are you there, over?" Parker spoke into the receiver.

"Ops com, copy," a voice crackled back.

Parker flipped through a checklist and began to relay his midday report. "DP, this is Harker, RTO one-six-eight-zero. I have alignment specs on birdhouse NE True, marker, four-one-one. Ticket two, uniform-kilo-lantern, one-four-three, over."

"One-four-three, copy," the operator, acknowledged.

"RP dumped. Active pinger set, five by one thousand – range one. Cold pots cracked and planted, marker Greenhouse Mallory. Close the file and activate modulation sequence, Foxtrot, over."

"Foxtrot initiated and your ticket is punched. Confirm acquisition of HE four-one-eight upon arrival, over."

"Copy, Midland."

"Check the board at nineteen-thirty for sector update, over."

"Eight-zero confirmed, good day."

"DP over and out," the voice fizzled.

Parker reclined into a restful position and took out a saved audio chip from Kiki, one that he would play every once in a while when he was feeling lonely. More than a month had passed since he heard any word from his sister and with the courier service being stretched thin, snippets and letters were now being delivered late and sporadically. He slipped the chip into the playback module of his com-link and listened to the recording.

Laughter and celebration echoed softly in the background before the jubilant voice of Kiki broke in. "Hey, Park! How ya doin'?" she began.

Jumbo's voice clamored. "Hey, buddy, where the hell are you? You're missing all the fun!"

"Get out of here," Kiki gleefully kidded. "He's just glad because he got bumped up to Flight Leader. Lucky duck… Now, where should I start? So much has happened since I last spoke to you. Wait, hang on a second."

The sound of a door closing could be heard and the raucous clamor of the festivity dimmed. "Sorry about that. Jumbo and the squadron are just celebrating. Strangely enough, it's actually for me. You see I got my first kill today. It was quite an experience, or so they say. To tell you the truth, I don't really remember much of it. There was a little puff of smoke, then… Poof. It was all over. I wish you could have seen it."

The recording fizzled out. When her voice returned, she sounded calmer and more subdued. She said softly, "Hi, I'm back. I know you don't approve of what I'm doing, but it was the right choice, for both of us. Maybe someday you'll understand. I'm sorry about the way I left and what I said. I didn't mean it. You're a good man, Park. I always knew you'd be there to take care of me and catch me when I fell. Even if you couldn't hold on to me, but that's another story," she giggled. "I'll always love you for that." There was a pause. "So, how are things back at home? I bet you're still busting your knuckles on that broken Hedgehog. That crackpot never worked. It's funny, though. Sometimes, I really miss that piece of junk. For some reason, when I was locked in that dogfight the other day, that memory popped into my head. I wonder if −" An alarm bell rang out in the background. "Oops, I've got to go! Wish me luck! I'll send you another snip when I have a chance. Miss ya." The message ended.

Parker reached into his vest pocket and retrieved Kiki's old tuning wrench. He twirled the metal spanner between his fingers and set his head against Old Gurdy. It felt good to hear his sister's voice and to know that she was alive and faring well. Tilting the brim of his hat over his face, Parker closed his eyes and folded his arms across his chest for a short midday nap.

A half-hour later, while Parker was asleep, that a strange pair of mechanical claws reached down from the canopy above. They were nimble and delicate and attached to a robotic creature that resembled something like a preying mantis. Its painted camouflage and swaying movement matched the texture and color of the oak tree's branches to perfection. The surveillance mech, commonly known as a "twig," lightly poked and prodded Parker's utility vest in an attempt to gather information. Irritated, Parker shooed the annoying pest with a wave of his hand. The twitchy robot jerked back momentarily before slowly moving in for a closer look with its mechanical eyes. With a few more light touches and strokes, the twig managed to pull Parker's hat from his face. Startled, Parker leaped up from the ground and stuttered, "Wh-what the…?" The mechanical creature again leaned in with curiosity and touched his face.

Parker slid up against the trunk of Old Gurdy until he was standing fully upright as the robot edged its needle-sharp appendages directly in front of his eyes. He tried desperately to call for help but managed only to squeak a meager "-elp."

Beyond the horizon, he heard barking and noticed a furry golden mass approaching from the periphery. In the distance, he heard the dog's owner whistling and shouting, "Stop! Hold on!"

The dog eagerly rushed up to Parker and began to sniff his feet.

The voice called out again. "Good boy! You found it."

From down the hill, a woman dressed in coveralls and utility fatigues neared the peculiar scene and seemed oblivious to Parker's plight. She was too busy gathering her bearings and navigating the terrain through a tiny topography sensor strapped around her wrist. She grabbed hold of the dog's harness and calmed him down with a gentle pat.

Meanwhile, the curious twig slowly began crawling down Parker's chest. He motioned his arm carefully to the side and finally managed to reach out and touch the young lady's hand with his fingers.

"Who's there?" she pulled away, startled.

Parker did his best to clear his throat and etch out a final call for help.

The woman reacted swiftly by punching in a series of commands into a remote that caused the inquisitive robot to immediately stop what it was doing and slip back into the leafy foliage.

"I'm terribly sorry," the young lady responded. "I didn't know anyone was here."

Parker peered up at the canopy for signs of the uninvited voyeur. "Me neither," he replied. "What was that?"

"Oh that. It's nothing. Just a Wolleby."

"A wola-what?"

"A Wolleby, a T. Westoleby surveillance mech. Tac calls them Twigs, but I think Wolleby sounds better. Don't you?"

"Uh, sure... Wait, it's a robot?"

"A mech. Robots are programmed, but mechs have flexible memory cores. I'm sorry if it frightened you. I sent out a carrier signal for some of the locals to rendezvous here."

"You mean there's more?"

"Plenty. There are Snuffs, Docs, Grazers, and as you've already met, Wollebies. There's an entire ecosystem abounding about these hills, but I wouldn't worry too much. They're scattered pretty thin."

"Not thin enough," Parker whispered under his breath.

The excited retriever sniffed Parker again before leaping up onto his chest and licking his face. The young lady pulled on his collar and scolded, "Smilie, stop that! What are you doing?"

"Smilie?"

"You're too old to be jumping up on people like that. What's gotten into you?"

Parker was astonished. "Could it be?" he wondered. He examined the woman more thoroughly. She seemed to be about the right age, though her voice was different and of course she was much older than the image in his memory. Then, in a flash, it struck him like a bolt of lightning. Captivated once again by the radiant beauty of this familiar stranger, he stuttered nervously, "T-T-Tilly?"

"Yes," she said.

Tilly also quickly came to realize whom it was she was talking to. "Parker? Parker, is that you?" she asked.

Parker reached out and embraced her in a joyful hug.

"What are you doing here?"

"I'm a transfer sent up here from Slewy."

Parker could hardly contain his excitement. "Wait, are you telling me you're the re-o that I put in for?"

"Well, if you're the sector specialist, I suppose I am."

"I don't believe this," he scratched his head. "It can't be. I'm not that lucky."

Tilly stood bashfully biting her lip. She was embarrassed to tell him the truth but decided to come clean. "Actually, Parker, you're not. The truth is, I've been trying to get back here for a long time. In fact, it's been so long I wasn't sure if I ever could. It was my dream to return to Kakkie. It's the only real home I ever had. When I overheard there was a Harker registered out here as a Radioman, I thought maybe… I didn't know if it was your father or someone else, but I thought I'd take a chance. I'm sure this sounds kind of crazy, but ever since the day I left, I've been trying hard to find you."

"Me?"

"I've missed you, Parker. You were my best friend and this place was the fondest memory I had growing up."

"But what about your aunt? And the Meadowlands?"

"I was only there a few months. After my uncle died, she wasn't the same anymore and she passed away shortly after. I guess it was just a little too much for her to bear," she said sadly. "After that, life got pretty tough, what with the rationing and all."

"Yeah," Parker nodded in agreement. He tried to find something appropriate to say but ended up settling on the generic, "I'm sorry."

"Don't be," Tilly smiled. "I'm not. The orphanage took care of me, educated me, trained me to become a tinker, and in a strange way brought me back here, back home. It's actually pretty amazing when you think about it." Stopping herself from becoming overly sentimental, she directed a question back at Parker, "But enough about me. What have you been up to? How's your father? And Kiki?"

Parker took a moment before answering. "My father was killed in a bombing raid."

Tilly was saddened by the tragic news. The never-ending war had taken many lives but death was never easy, especially when it was someone she knew.

"And as for Kiki," Parker continued, "she's trying hard to follow in his footsteps."

Confused, Tilly replied, "I'm sorry, I don't think I follow. Did I miss something?"

Parker explained, "She and Jumbo went off to join Air Armory. For some reason she thinks that she can avenge death by doing a little killing of her own."

"It sounds like you don't approve."

"I don't," Parker stated frankly.

"Well, Kiki's a sneak. I'm sure she'll pull through. She always finds a way to land on her feet."

"I hope you're right, but I think that cat might have climbed up a tree that's just too high." Parker looked up to the sky and wondered where his sister might be at that moment. A myriad of emotions ran through his mind. He felt torn between the joy he felt at being reunited with his childhood sweetheart and the fear that plagued him when he thought about his sister's safety. He took a deep breath before turning his attention back to Tilly. "It's nice to see you again, Till."

"Thanks," she smiled. "It's nice to be back."

The Radioman felt his presence drift back into the confines of the Doc's laboratory. His arms and legs pulled taut, his body was now fully extended along the cold examination table. Lines of intravenous tubes ran channels of elixirs through his forearm, and he could feel a damp stickiness from the electrodes that were taped along his chest and forehead. No longer, however, could he see his captor.

The Doc's face and bulbous hunchback were now shrouded in darkness. Only the edges of his massive arm could be seen. The Doc's wrinkled hand reached for a dial next to the Radioman's head and turned it clockwise. An electrical buzz began to hum. The hand then reached for a lever and pulled it down to complete an electrical circuit.

A wave of pain rushed through the Radioman's temples as the darkness gave way to light. The blurred image of green and brown once again filled his mind and sharpened into focus.

It was late autumn. The days were getting shorter and an early morning shower had dampened the already saturated ground, making conditions a very sloppy affair. Thin trails of matted grass spread out like tentacles of an octopus that led to and from each of the towering monoliths that dotted the Kakydurn landscape.

Through the slippery mud, Parker and Tilly made their way toward an anti-aircraft slinger located near the Hipper Flats. The trek was long and slow, but neither seemed to mind as both were smitten in the company of each other.

When they finally arrived at the installation, both were in need of a moment's rest. Smilie, on the other hand, was still full of energy and reveling in the soft and slushy soil. Stepping up onto the artillery's concrete base, Parker reached back to lend Tilly a hand. He unbuckled his heavy utility belt and set it down onto the platform as Tilly popped open a hydro-canister filled with tea.

"Thirsty?" she asked.

"No thanks. You go ahead," Parker replied as he scanned for signs of a courier drop. "This is the right unit. I wonder where the shipment is?" Flipping down his optics, he spotted a wooden crate sliding down the muddy slope toward the sea. "Nuts! There it is," he said worriedly. "Look, why don't you take a break before setting up shop. I'm going to get a jump on hauling those ammo bricks up here before they go for a swim."

"Do you need help?"

"No, I'll be fine."

Parker leaned over and gave Tilly a peck on the forehead before dashing to retrieve the parcel. "Be back in a snip."

By the time Parker finished moving the boxes of ammo up to the slinger, it was well after noon and despite his body feeling sore and fatigued, he immediately began loading the chrome-plated darts into the cannon's feed mechanism. He figured it was best to finish the job in a single outing rather than having to slog back out in the muck the following day. Packing in the last of the rounds, Parker closed the magazine cover and strapped on his utility belt. Crawling up to the top of the mighty behemoth, he straddled the cannon's barrel and began work on the battery's targeting sensor.

As Tilly wrapped up work on the line of mechs that had gathered around her makeshift outpost, a small field medic labored its way up the hill. The "Doc," as it was commonly known, grinded achingly as its split wheel of propulsion struggled to spin through the layers of mud and debris that had become jammed between its corrugated tracks and axle bearings.

Making it to the base of the slinger, Smilie ran over and sniffed the Doc's spherical head curiously as it powered down, exhausted. Tilly pulled a cable from her diagnostic translator and plugged it into the communication port located along the mech's reflective dome. Once connected, the Doc let out a series of beeps and clicks to inform Tilly of its troubles.

"I don't know, little fella," Tilly replied. "That's a pretty tall order."

The Doc chirped another series of binary taps.

Tilly understood what the robot needed and informed, "I can do a couple of minor patches and maybe free up that sprocket, but, mind you, that gear box is leaking oil and you'll need to get a permanent fix at a staging center."

The Doc bowed its head in agreement as Tilly began making the necessary repairs.

Medical Mech
"Doc"

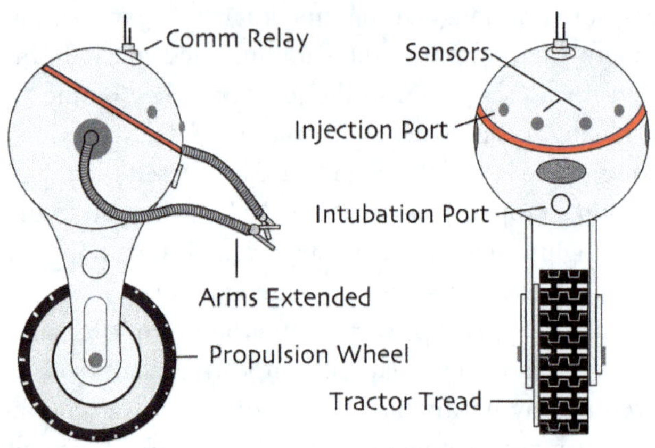

It wasn't long before the Doc was up and running again. Tilly finished by polishing off the last remnants of crusted soil from the robot's muted veneer.

"There you go, little guy," she smiled.

The mech chirped in appreciation.

"Try to tread lightly until you can get a proper mend. And don't forget to tell the techs to get a fresh load of grease on those cogs and to adjust that drive-side tension pulley.

The Doc noted the suggestions into his memory banks and beeped a friendly "Thank you" before scurrying off back into the grass.

"I'm finished down here," Tilly called up at Parker. "How are you coming along?"

Parker latched down the cover of an access panel. "Almost done, I just got one more coil to–"

Without warning, the anti-aircraft unit suddenly came online and burst into life. Parker wrapped his arms and legs around the barrel as it bucked and thrashed him once to the left and then to the right. The cannon's pneumatic compressor quickly charged to capacity as it prepared for an attack. In a final jolt, the slinger flung Parker high into the air and he splashed onto the muddy ground, his tools strewn about in a chaotic mess. The acquisition sequence complete, the first dart in the magazine chambered into the cannon's breech and exploded out the barrel.

A pair of Crinch bombers wisped speedily through the clouds above as the slinger traced a line of destruction across the sky. The explosive shells puffed like kernels of popcorn against the grey sky and struck the lead bomber with a direct hit. The aircraft disintegrated into a ball of flame that sent huge chunks of shrapnel colliding into the trailing bomber, crippling its engines. A caustic stream of black smoke spewed from the second bomber as it sputtered downward over the crest of a nearby hill.

Parker listened as echoes of a crash reverberated through the air.

"Jiggers!" Parker shouted.

"What was that?" Tilly asked.

"Come on!"

Parker grabbed Tilly by the arm and rushed over to the site where the enemy had landed.

Along an empty field, the trio came across the fuselage of the crumpled bomber. A gully of charred metal led a path of wreckage more than a hundred meters long. Parker spotted the dead body of a pilot slumped over an instrument panel. As he panned across, he noticed a crimson trail of blood smeared along the wet grass that disappeared behind the wreckage.

It was then that Parker heard a scream. He angled around to get a better view and spotted the second member of the crew locked in battle with a mechanical grazer. Slashed at the legs by the mechs' sharpened claws, the pilot fell to the ground, shrieking in painful agony.

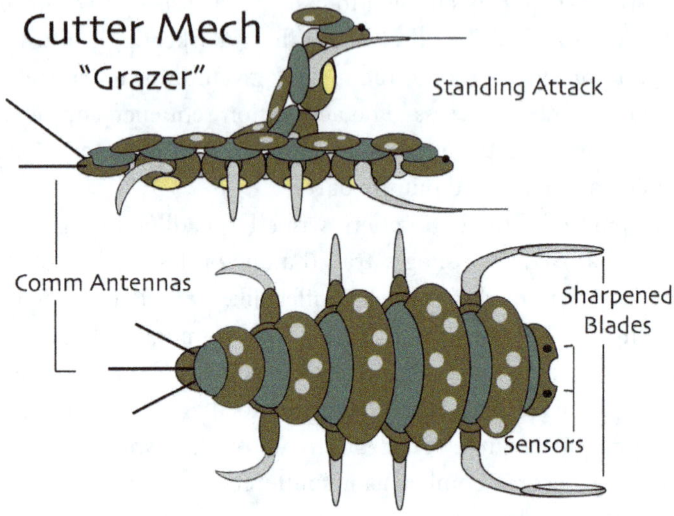

Smilie growled as the grisly drama played out before him. The tiny robot spun around with its bloodied appendages raised high in the air, and scanned the retriever for identification. Quickly, it confirmed the canine as being friendly and turned back to resume its attack.

Tilly commanded, "Smilie, stop!"

The wounded pilot pulled a sidearm from his holster and fumbled to aim the pistol. Lowering the sights onto the grazer, he pulled the trigger.

The bullet ripped a gaping hole through the assassin's metal armor and the robot wheezed a series of blips and squeaks before collapsing in a sizzling puddle of charged hydraulic fluid. Though severely injured, the crippled man managed to drag himself along the slippery turf away from the crash site.

As the ghastly scene unfolded, Parker could feel a wave of panic surge from within. He wanted desperately to end the pilot's suffering, but years of war and death reminded him that this man was the enemy and it was the network's job to defend its territory against the Crinch.

Still, something touched him deep inside. He wasn't sure if it was fear or sympathy, but the intense feeling drove him to take action.

"Stay here," he instructed Tilly. "I'll be right back!"

"No, wait!" Tilly warned. "It's not safe!" Her words, however, went unheard as Parker was already in full stride.

As he passed through the cloud of black smoke spewing from the engine's exhaust, he could see the pilot crawling along the ground.

Parker heard the sound of a mortar pop and noticed something cylindrical bounce into the air just ahead of the pilot. The tiny snuff spun wildly and screeched to a high-pitched crescendo.

Tilly shouted at the top of her lungs, "Parker, get down!"

Parker covered his head and dropped to the ground. A thunderous explosion followed and he was knocked unconscious.

When Parker came to, his head throbbed and there was a deafening ring in his ears. He opened his eyes groggily and saw Tilly mouthing words that sounded muted and muffled.

"Parker? Parker? Are you all right?"

"What happened?" he asked, rubbing his temples.

"You were one foolhardy leap from getting snuffed."

As he took a moment to gather his bearings, a final mech made its way to the crash site. The recently repaired Doc delicately approached the body of the fallen enemy. It was then that Parker smelled the sickening stench of burnt flesh. He turned away from the gruesome sight and covered his nose and mouth with his hand.

"Poor bastard," he muttered.

The Doc worked quickly to save what was left of the convulsing carcass. It sprayed a coating of antibacterial gel over the open wounds and injected a series of chemical elixirs to help stabilize the man's condition. Despite the Doc's best efforts, it was too late. As a final measure, the Doc inserted a respiration valve into the enemy pilot's body via a thin flexible tube. The pilot's chest heaved, trying to hold on to his last moments of life.

His eyes pressed shut, Parker suddenly heard a startling cry. He peeked through his fingers and met the eyes of the dying pilot staring back at him. He could see the gray of death shading over the pilot's dilating pupils and noticed the rhythmic gaping of his lips as he struggled for air. Parker watched as each of the pilot's labored breaths transformed into an epic battle to stay alive. Through the struggling gasps, Kiki's voice suddenly appeared in the midst of the man's last exhalation.

"Save me," her voice echoed.

His eyes filled with tears, Parker burst out shouting, "No!"

Confused by all the commotion, Tilly grabbed Parker by the arm, "What's going on? What's wrong?"

"Stop it!" he screamed. "Make it stop!"

Tilly held him tightly as the terrifying ordeal finally came to an end.

With all the Doc's resources exhausted, it detached the sensors and probes and stood motionless for a time. The mech seemed almost human as it grieved sadly over the loss.

Sensing the struggle was over. Tilly said reassuringly, "It's all right, Parker. It's over."

The Doc rested a small homing beacon on top of the tattered corpse and quietly rolled back into the grass.

Holding Parker's hand, Tilly asked, "Are you okay?"

Parker was calmer now, but what he just witnessed had triggered a sorrow and hopelessness that he could feel in every cell of his being. He recalled the death of his parents and the lost innocence of childhood. He yearned for the warmth of the earlier days when the world was safe and wanted now more than ever to feel secure once again. He grabbed Tilly and began to weep. He desperately wanted something permanent to hold onto, something that would anchor him and let him know he was not alone. Shivering, he cupped Tilly's face with his hands and whispered, "Marry me?"

Tilly was caught by surprise. "What did you say?"

"I want to marry you. That is, if you'll have me. I don't want to be alone anymore."

"But I –"

"–Please," Parker pleaded. "We could head down to Bix and get hitched over at the Breyer. I've got some time saved up and maybe we could make it out to March for a little R&R."

Tilly was speechless, her mind in a tizzy.

"I've been so scared and miserable for so long that I forgot what it is to have a dream." Parker held Tilly's hands tightly. "But I know now. I know what it is that I've been missing... It's you."

An awkward silence fell upon the moment and soon Parker realized he must have frightened Tilly. Disappointment and embarrassment trickled like drops of molten lead as he released his grip and wiped the tears from his eyes. Then, mustering as much dignity as he could, he apologized. "I'm sorry, Till. I guess I got a little caught up in the moment. I hope I didn't scare you."

Sadly, Parker leaned down and picked up his work spectacles before brushing the mud from his trousers.

As he turned to leave, Tilly reached over and responded softly, "I will."

In an instant, Parker felt as if a great burden had been lifted. That simple touch, those two words, filled him with happiness and joy. He threw his arms around Tilly and squeezed her tight.

"Thank you," he beamed.

Amidst the death and destruction that marked their fateful passage through this turbulent time, Parker and Tilly stood embraced, their hearts filled with the promise of brighter days to come.

It was two weeks later when the happy couple returned from their honeymoon. Dressed in civilian clothes, the couple seemed merrily adjusted to their new roles as husband and wife and for the first time in a long time, Parker felt refreshed and relaxed.

Along the front porch, a small weather-beaten package wrapped in plain brown paper had been left at the entry. With Tilly in his arms and Smilie by his side, Parker unlatched the front door and shuffled the small box across the threshold with his foot.

He set Tilly down gently on her feet and said cheerfully, "Welcome home, Mrs. Harker."

"Home," she repeated. "Who would have thought such a simple word could sound so nice?"

Parker picked up the package and set it upon the mantle. Leading Tilly on a brief tour of the hovel, they eventually made their way to the bedroom. Parker rushed to shuffle a stack of boxes to a corner and apologized, "Sorry the place is such a mess. I probably should have tidied it up before we left, but at the time I didn't know I would be gaining a new roommate."

"I think the term most people use is 'wife.'"

"Oh, right. Wife. I still can't believe we're actually married. If you give me a few minutes, I'll clear up some space."

"Don't bother. I don't have much. But Smilie, on the other hand… That pup sure likes to shuffle his bones," Tilly kidded.

Parker didn't get the joke and looked over at Smilie for some help, but his inquiry was met with a shared look of confusion.

Wiping the wrinkles from the bedding, the two newlyweds fell onto the mattress with their legs dangling off the edge of the bed.

"It's nice here," Tilly snuggled up to Parker. "Cozy."

Parker gazed upon Tilly's soft profile. "I wish this moment would last forever." He leaned in and kissed her gently on the lips.

Tilly reveled in the thought that her long days of yearning were now nothing more than a distant memory and all her dreams had finally come true.

A draft blew in from the entry, where the door was left open. Shivering, Parker said to Tilly, "Why don't you rest here. I'll go start a fire and put a kettle on."

Exiting the bedroom, he walked back out to the porch to gather some wood. Opening the flue on the chimney, he lit a tuft of dry grass under a small pile of kindling and waited for the sticks to catch fire. As the hearth began to radiate heat, Parker warmed his hands against the flames.

He spotted the tightly wrapped parcel resting along the mantle directly in front of him. Parker had received hundreds of similar packages before. Usually, they were stuffed with a new spigot, spare part, or replacement I.D. He picked it up and untied the twine that was sealed around the edges. He tore away the shipping paper and tossed it into the fire. What remained was a small wooden box with a glass lid. "What's this?" he wondered.

Peering through the cover, he noticed a pewter pendant with painted white feathers mounted on a sheet of cardboard. He lifted the wing-shaped insignia up for a closer look. There was a neatly folded letter attached to the underside of the box. Parker unfolded the official letterhead and read the note out loud: "We regret to inform you that − PILOT OFFICER KIKI HARKER − has been listed MISSING IN ACTION while in the service of AIR ARMORY…"

Shocked, Parker uttered, "No, it can't be. This has to be a mistake. This can't be true."

The wooden case slipped from his fingers.

In the bedroom, Tilly and Smilie were stirred by the sound of shattering glass. "Is everything all right? Parker?" Tilly asked.

Parker did not answer. His heart pounding, he felt an uncontrollable urge to flee. He gripped the pendant in his hand and dashed out of the hovel.

Under the glow of a crescent moon, Parker found himself miles from the village. Through the milky haze of fog, he could see the outline of the Chatley Ruins standing before him. He scaled to the top and took a seat along the same archway that he and his sister sat on before as children. He clutched the wings tightly and shouted into the darkness, "Kiki, where are you? I told you not to go! Why didn't you listen to me?"

Parker was unable to control his emotions – his fear turned to anger and he wanted revenge. He wanted to pummel something. He wanted to find whoever it was that was responsible for this injustice and force them to share his pain. But looking out into the darkness, he saw no one, not a single soul, only the cold walls of the abandoned persey reflecting shades of gray.

Eventually, the quiet night tempered his rage and he was left feeling empty and confused. As the hours passed, Parker slowly came to accept that Kiki was gone.

"A missing person is a dead person," Parker told himself. "Missing only means they couldn't find a body or there was nothing left to find."

Still, for some unexplainable reason, something from within betrayed him. Maybe it was that single word "missing" that kept him clinging to the prospect of his sister's return, or maybe because the truth was just too difficult to accept. In any case, because of that tiny shred of hope, Parker could not let her go.

"She's not dead," Parker told himself. "Just like Tilly said earlier, Kiki always finds a way to land on her feet. But where could she be?"

He fixated his mind on the slimmest of possibilities. He remembered the promise that he had made to his father, a promise that for the moment had been broken. In an instant, the world felt too large to fathom and too painful to endure. He wanted to escape, to be free from the fear that always kept him dreadful of the future. In the end, however, Parker realized he was just one person trapped in a conflict of many – an insignificant player no more important than a speck of dust resting atop an old relic, trying desperately to hold onto a past that could not be recovered.

Rays of early morning sunlight broke over the horizon and warmed Parker's face. He opened his swollen eyes and saw the valley below blanketed in a dense fog that glowed luminously.

In the distance, two figures trekked across the hillside. It was a vision he recalled from memory: the Griffin and the Ghost.

He wondered if his mind might be playing tricks on him. He rubbed his bloodshot eyes to help sharpen the image, but when he looked back, the phantoms were no longer there. "I must be dreaming," he thought. "This damn cold is muddling my mind."

Parker looked down at the metal pendant clutched within his palm. He took a deep breath of brisk morning air and tried to focus his thoughts back on his sister. "You're not dead, Kiki. I can feel it. Just as sure as I know myself, I know you're alive."

A feeling of newfound hope energized Parker and he felt his luck had changed. He conjured up a plan of action and declared, "Against the odds, Tilly found me and I'll find you." It all seemed so simple. "Recover that which is lost and set the world to rights." This became Parker's new mantra, one he repeated over and over in his mind as he committed his life to a destiny unknown.

Though he knew Tilly was waiting back at the hovel, Parker felt compelled to act before he had a chance to second-guess his decision. He knew that if he didn't, he might soon lose the courage to follow in his sister's footsteps.

Venturing down to the Mumpy Grove, Parker entered a tree-lined gully that channeled between two adjoining hills. The steep ravine of jagged fissures formed a natural stronghold against aerial bombardment.

Deep within the underbrush, Parker came across a sealed entrance that led to the sector's defense operations center, known as Daisy Point. He pulled down on a release handle but found the door locked. From under his foot, the top of a robot snuff popped up from the ground and scanned him for identification.

Parker was quite wary of this mech, and rightly so, for he had seen firsthand the damage the suicidal robot could inflict. He stood still as the snuff concentrated its attention on his closed fist and chirped a few bars of binary code. Parker responded by revealing the small pendant clutched within his palm. The snuff cross-referenced the emblem as friendly and quietly tumbled away.

Parker tapped the access panel once more, but again nothing happened.

"What's going on?" he wondered.

He ran the procedure through his mind several more times, until it dawned on him that he was out of uniform and was being denied access because he did not have a single piece of identification on his person.

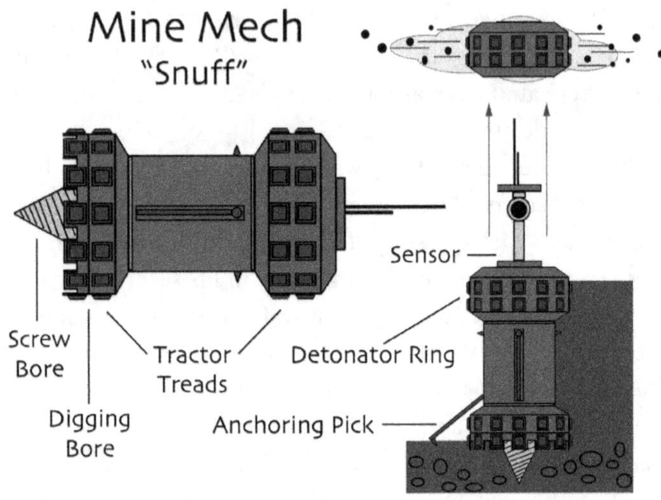

An eerie chill ran through him when he realized just how close he had come to being killed. Exhaling with relief, he knew it was probably Kiki's tarnished wings that saved his life. He gripped them just a little tighter before dialing in for an operator.

"DP, are you there?"

A voice rang out from an overhead speaker. "This is Hot Dog Seven, over."

"HD, this is RTO one-six-eight-zero," Parker replied. "I need a security override at checkpoint MG Alpha, over."

"Eight-zero, copy. T & T confirm?"

"Nut Grinder. Tally, thirty-one kilo."

A moment later, the deadbolt solenoids clicked open and unlocked the heavily reinforced door.

Parker kicked the mud from his shoes and dusted off his trousers before stepping inside. He headed down a long corridor that emerged into a massive underground rotunda.

Edging up against a handrail, he peered down to the theater below and saw an enormous topographical map of the sector surrounded by a group of operators. The map was dotted with markers that identified every sonar tower, thumper, slinger, and transmission array erected within the region, while specialized technicians monitored the constant influx of reports and dispatches that inundated the network.

At the far end of the auditorium, tucked away in a corner, Parker spotted an old friend from field training, a sonar operator nicknamed Hunch. He was a jolly fellow with a thick neck and who wore equally thick spectacles. Parker slipped his way through the hustle and bustle and tapped Hunch on the shoulder. A hand swung swiftly upward, signaling not to be disturbed. Parker leaned in to view a display filled with a pattern of slow-moving green lines. The chubby specialist tuned in on an enemy contact with a twist of a knob. Cupping his hands over the headsets, Hunch focused with keen concentration.

Once able to zero in on the signal, he snapped his fingers and shouted to a nearby dispatcher, "Echo contact! Grid three, eight, five, heading southwest at flight level zero, two thousand! Looks like a single. Ring up CC Keller for intercept and tell them to be on the lookout for a live one."

The dispatcher nodded and proceeded to send out the alert.

Hunch reclined back in his chair and pulled the headsets down around his neck. Rubbing the tension from the bridge of his nose, he adjusted his glasses before turning his attention to Parker. He was surprised to see his friend back from leave so soon but greeted him happily with a firm handshake. "Hey there, Park. What are you doing here? I thought you were on leave."

"I just got back." Parker looked down a darkened corridor and asked, "Is he in?"

"Oh, he's in," Hunch warned. "Buried deep and simmering nicely. If I were you, I'd probably check in later."

"Unfortunately, this can't wait."

"Well, it's your hide," Hunch shrugged. "Don't say I didn't warn you."

Parker patted Hunch on the back. "Wish me luck."

Hunch shook his head as he placed the headsets back over his ears.

Peering down the hall, Parker cautiously proceeded toward the Station Master's ready room.

Seeing the door left slightly ajar, Parker knocked timidly before entering. Quietly, he stepped in and noticed Field Commander Veil sitting with his back turned and his chin nestled in the palm of his hand.

A voice muttered, "Unless that door was blown open by my dead mother's ghost, you better start talking."

Hunch was right. The CO was in a terrible mood and Parker considered backing away before being spotted.

The weary commander grumbled, "Just give it to me straight. What's broken and how long until we can get it back up?"

Parker knew this was definitely the wrong time to be asking for any favors so he decided to duck out. However, just as he began to edge his way from the door, the commander spun around and shouted, "Damn it! If you've got something to say, say it! I've got a sector to run!"

Parker immediately snapped himself to attention.

Veil quickly identified Parker as someone useful and changed his tone, "Oh, it's you. I didn't know you were back. Didn't I sign you off on a two-week pass? Getting married, as I recall. Why anyone would want to get hitched during this miserable war, I'll never know."

"Yes, sir. Married," Parker nodded. "But I got in last night."

Veil perked up. "That's great!"

From his desk drawer, the CO procured a bottle of brill and poured a pair of drinks.

Raising his glass, he cleared his throat and peered at a picture on his desk. In a somber tone, he toasted, "To our better halves. I hope it works out for you."

Swilling the sharp liquor, Parker felt his innards clench as the alcohol warmed his empty stomach. Commander Veil then slid the bottle aside and focused on the task at hand.

"I'm glad you're back. You're just the man I wanted to see. I've got a botched slinger out in Wex that could use a bit of love. The tinker out there is bottomed out for at least a week. I can spring you a duck and have you out there within the hour. It's a short hop and with your skills, you ought to have that slinger hurling by sundown."

"Actually, sir," Parker nervously interrupted. "To tell you the truth, I'm here to ask you for a favor."

"A favor? What kind of favor? If it's about the schedule, I can't give you any more time off. At least not until the end of the season when all new the pots are planted."

"No, sir, it's not that. I want to request a transfer."

"Transfer?" The CO was taken aback. "Now, hang on a minute." He rocked back in his chair. "Was it something I said?"

"No, sir. It's a bit of a story and kind of hard to explain."

"Look, I know you're all hopped up on hormones right now, but I'm in deep. The Ruddy are trying to bust a line through detection from Tenory to Tumblerland. I'll make a deal with you. If you can get that slinger back up, I'll try and pull some strings to get you an extra couple of days off before you get back into the loop."

"Sir, I want to take a shot at Air Armory."

"ARM?" Commander Veil looked puzzled.

"Yes, sir. I'm H-Op qualified and I think I have enough booked time to make grade. But any recommendation from you would be a great help in expediting the transition."

The CO leaned forward and rested his elbows on the desk. "Why the hell would you want to transfer? You've got a good thing going here. You're a wiz at your job, and besides that you're home-front." He rubbed his temples and cursed, "Jiggers."

"Sir, you've always been fair with me. And I wouldn't ask if it wasn't really important."

The CO poured himself another drink. "First your sister and now you. What is it with you kids?" He tossed back the brill. "Harker, you're the best tech I've got. And believe me, I've seen a few come through in my time. Just how do you think I'm going to keep this place patched together without you?"

"I can update Underhill and Sparky on the new partitions and make sure they each get a rundown of my route until you can get a re-o dispatched."

The CO scratched his head. He asked once more, "Why do you want to go and fly around with those buzzards anyway?"

"Believe me, sir. I'm no fan of heights, but it's something I have to do."

"Look, maybe you should take a couple days to think it over. Talk it over with the missus."

"Thank you, sir. But I've made up my mind."

Commander Veil frowned in defeat. "Damn Air Ministry. They get all the priority." He slid the bottle back into his desk drawer and shook his head in disappointment. "Why the Primes are so eager to push this thing in the air, I have no idea. Are you certain you don't want a transfer to Observation or Records? I can stall that rotation for years."

"Yes, I'm sure."

Understanding he most likely couldn't stop Parker from leaving, he tried to swing a deal. "All right, I'll tell you what," the CO conceded. "You get out there and patch up that slinger, and if your decision doesn't change by the time you get back, I'll punch it through."

"Thank you, sir. I appreciate it."

"Don't thank me. I'm not doing you any favors. It's no picnic up there. From what I hear, they're dropping like flies. I just hope you know what you're doing."

Parker nodded uneasily, wondering himself if it was a wise decision.

"We're really going to miss your handiwork around here," Veil said, reaching out to shake Parker's hand. "You're one of kind, Harker. A real frequency junkie, a natural born radioman."

It was evening when Parker finally returned home. His body was exhausted from the long day of traveling and fixing the broken slinger. And despite all the time he had to prepare for his conversation with Tilly, he still hadn't figured out a way to break the news.

As he removed his shoes and set them against the entry, a voice called from the kitchen.

"Parker? Is that you?"

"Yes," he replied.

"Are you all right?" Tilly asked. "You left without saying a word. And when you didn't come back last night, I wasn't sure what happened."

"I'm sorry, Till. I didn't mean to worry you. I was out at Wex. There was a bit of an emergency."

"Something serious?"

"No, just a botched slinger."

A gentle aroma wafted in from the kitchen and Parker took the opportunity to change the subject.

"What's that smell?"

"Oh, it's a cake. I was hoping to celebrate," Tilly explained.

"Celebrate what?"

"I'll tell you later. Let's eat."

She took Parker's hand and slowly guided him to take a seat at the dining table. He was amazed how well Tilly had adjusted to her new surroundings and couldn't understand how she was able to prepare food without being able to see.

"This is quite a surprise," Parker said. "You know, cooking is hard enough for me, but I can't figure out how you managed to–"

"–Bake it? Oh, it's just one of those box rations. I found it sitting in the back of the pantry. If I concentrate hard enough, I can sometimes make out a few things up close. The world through my eyes is like looking through a blanket of fog. Everything's soft and fuzzy."

Parker leaned in for a closer look at the fluffy yellow loaf steaming in its hot square tin. "Well, it looks great!" Parker complimented.

"Yes, but how does it taste?"

"It looks almost too good to eat."

"Well, cakes are meant to be eaten, that's their purpose. You wouldn't want to go and disappoint the little fella now, would you?"

"Of course not."

Sliding in a knife, he carved out a small slice and lifted it from the pan. He broke the piece in two and fed half to Tilly. As he indulged in the delicate sweetness, memories of his own mother's baking warmed him from within. The buttery flavor lingered on his tongue and he nodded approvingly. "It's delicious."

"I'm glad you like it," Tilly felt a sense of accomplishment.

Parker looked upon his new bride with feelings of guilt and sadness. He thought it ironic that after all these years of waiting to live a life of happiness together, it was he who was about to alter the course of the future and set their lives upon a different path. He kissed Tilly tenderly on the lips.

"Thank you," he said fondly.

"It's just a cake," she giggled.

Following their evening meal, Parker, Tilly, and Smilie took a stroll up to the north end of the village where the grid's pneumatic power station was erected. The walk, he thought, would give him some extra time to find a way to explain to Tilly the reason for his imminent departure.

As they arrived at the wind farm, an offshore breeze blew in from the coast. Through the labyrinth of corrugated walkways, the trio made their way to an observation platform that jutted high above the valley below. The humming generators purred like kittens at their feet and Tilly noted playfully, "It tickles."

Parker rested his elbows against a hand railing and stared out towards the sea. He was beginning to have reservations about his rash decision to leave and thought, "Maybe it's just a pipe dream. Even if Kiki is still alive, how will I ever be able to find her?"

From the elevated vantage point, Parker shifted his gaze downward and saw the village of Kakydurn twinkling in the darkness.

"What does it look like?" Tilly asked. "The village. What does it look like from here?"

"Well, have you ever seen a pearl?" he began.

Tilly nodded her head.

"It's a bit like that. It glows like a jewel. Translucent, soft, like a child nestled in its mother's arms."

"That's nice," Tilly smiled as she ran her hand gently across her belly.

A silence settled between the two as each seemed to be deep in thought. After a moment, they turned to face each other and blurted in unison, "I need to tell you something!"

They laughed at the coincidence before Tilly politely deferred. "You go first."

"Okay," Parker said, clearing his throat. "I'm sure it must have seemed kind of strange last night, me leaving so suddenly. But I had just received some rather shocking news."

"I figured it must have been something pretty important."

"It was a message from Sector Command up at Squeller. They reported that Kiki was shot down while on patrol."

"Oh, Parker, I'm so sorry. Are you okay? Is there anything I can do?"

"Just one thing."

"Anything."

"I need you to understand."

"Understand what?

Parker brushed Tilly's hair to the side and took hold of her hands. "My decision to leave."

"What do you mean?"

"I'm transferring out."

"Transferring, where?"

"I'm getting a kick upstairs to do a rotation with Air Armory."

"But why? I thought the message said Kiki was killed."

"No, they only listed her as missing."

"Parker, I don't think that—"

"—No, she's alive!" Parker insisted. "I can feel it. Just as sure as I stand here now, I know she's alive!"

"Believe me, Parker. I know how hard it is to accept the loss of someone close, especially when there's no evidence or proof. But you can't live your life chasing after a ghost."

"It's not like that. Kiki's a sneak. You said so yourself. She always finds a way out."

"And I wish it were true, but you can't cheat death. And following in her footsteps isn't going to bring her back."

"Don't say that!" Parker shouted. "I will find her. I will!" A look of agony furrowed across Parker's face. "Besides, what choice do I have?"

"You have all the choices in the world," Tilly tried to reason with him. "We're married now. I want you to stay here with me so that we can build a life together. And with a bit of luck, grow old together."

"But I made a promise. I'm responsible for her."

"You did the best you could. You took care of her through the toughest of times. I'm sure of that. But that time has passed. She gone now, and eventually you have to let her go."

"I can't. She's my sister."

"And I'm your wife. You made a promise to me, too. I need you here, now, more than ever. I know this sounds selfish, but I've waited so long to be happy. And now that I've finally found some semblance of peace, some small corner of the world I can call my own, you tell me that you're leaving?" Tilly turned away, shielding her tears from Parker. "It's just not fair."

"But that's why of all people, I thought you would understand. You kept hope alive for all those years for a dream that you didn't think possible."

Smilie, knowing nothing of the history or events that had led to this irreconcilable moment, cocked his head quirkily as if trying to solve a riddle.

Parker leaned in and touched Tilly gently on the shoulder.

"Come on, Till," he comforted. "Everything's going to be fine, you'll see. After training and booking a bit of time, I'll figure it out. Just like you did. And I'll be back here before you know it. Please believe me. I would never purposely hurt you. You're all I ever wanted. I love –"

Tilly stopped him. "–Don't! Don't say it. If you have to go, then go. But don't say things that you don't mean."

Parker removed his hand and apologized, "I'm sorry."

Parker knew there would be no compromise that would warrant any further discussion. He had hurt Tilly enough with his decision, but it was final.

As he turned to leave, Tilly said. "Parker, I won't be there when you leave."

With nothing left to say, Parker journeyed back to the hovel alone to gather his gear and close his files.

Parker arrived at the landing zone early the next morning. He left well before daybreak when Tilly and Smilie were still asleep. As the muted sun broke over the horizon, an overcast sky spread a blanket of gray that engulfed the landscape as far as the eye could see. Slick morning dew covered the grassy field and made conditions appear even gloomier.

The sound of a transport roared in from above. Through the thick layer of clouds, it slowly dissolved into view and hovered in for a landing. "This is it," Parker told himself as blasts of compressed air released from the ship's blower as it touched down on the soft turf. He took a last lingering look at the misty landscape as the doors on the passenger pod slowly opened. A flood of memories filled his mind when he caught sight of Old Gurdy standing solitary with its roots anchored firmly to the ground. This place, these hills, marked the only home that Parker had ever known.

The sound of Smilie's barking pierced the air and snapped Parker out of his trance. Through the fog, he spotted the lively retriever scampering wildly toward him with Tilly in tow.

"Wait, Parker! Stop!" Tilly shouted. "Don't leave yet!"

Parker forced a melancholy smile as the two reached him, both out of breath. He rubbed Smilie on the head before taking Tilly into his arms.

"I thought you said you weren't going to come."

Tilly wiped tears from her face and kissed him passionately on the lips. "I lied."

"I love you," Parker said, holding her tightly. "Someday, I'll make it up to you."

"Just promise me you'll come back."

"I will," he said, kissing her deeply one last time.

The turbines roared back to life and a porter motioned Parker to climb aboard.

Stepping back from the entry, the hydraulic clamshell doors sealed shut and Tilly clasped her arms around Smilie as the transport lifted from the ground and drifted out of sight.

Drip, drip, drip. Cool droplets of condensation tapped against the Radioman's face and jostled him awake. Drenched in perspiration, his head throbbed with pulsating pressure. A scratchy dryness in his throat compelled him to angle his head sideways in an attempt to swallow a few drops of water into his mouth. His body shivered feverishly against the cold metal slab, while nearby he could hear the Doc stirring a solution.

From out of the darkness, the Doc leaned in and placed a hand on his shoulder. "You're doing fine," he comforted.

"Cold," the Radioman shuddered.

The Doc patted his forehead with a dampened towel before disappearing back into the void. "Just close your eyes and dream," his voice echoed.

A sharp prick from another injection entered his arm, and the Radioman felt a rush of warmth intoxicate his body.

WINTER

It had been four months since Parker left Kakydurn and he now stood in a line of a hundred new pilots. This group represented the Maver Air Proving Ground's winter class of graduates. White clouds drifted across the sky, casting a delicate pattern of shadow and light through the swaying fields of green. Next to Parker was his flight school bunkmate, Rex, who was currently in the process of having a set of wings pinned to his uniform. Teased as a child for a distinctive birthmark that encircled the left side of his face like a bull's eye, Rex now happily embraced the darkened patch and canine nickname that once haunted him as a child. Short in stature but bursting with energy, Rex was a naturally cheerful chap and the type of person who was always buzzing with optimism and eager to get into the mix. Grinning from ear to ear, he could not hide his excitement as Air Primary Weatherly snapped the retaining clip on the medallion and took a step back to salute the young man's promotion.

Next in line was Parker who clenched Kiki's wings nervously as an assistant opened a small wooden box and handed Weatherly the glistening pendant. However, as the

AP leaned in to pin on his award, Parker politely gestured to him to stop and revealed Kiki's wings cupped within his palm.

"Pardon me, sir. But if it's all the same, would you mind awarding me these?"

Air Primary Weatherly looked over at the tarnished pendant and commented, "They look a little roughed up and could use a bit of polish." He asked, "Your father's?"

"My sister's."

"Just as well," the AP acknowledged and placed the pendant snuggly against Parker's uniform. Stepping back, he saluted and moved on to the next graduate.

Parker gently motioned his hand over his heart and tapped the freshly pinned wings with the tips of his fingers.

The soft triumphant melody of Leialil's national anthem rose in the background as the class of newly indoctrinated pilots turned to face the nation's banner fluttering in the breeze. For the first time in his life, Parker understood the feelings of patriotism and purpose that had enticed Kiki and Jumbo to leave their home – for in this brief moment, he, too, was swept up in the seductive allure of splendor and glory that would often trap soldiers of war.

That evening, when all the pomp and circumstance had ended, Parker took a walk across the airfield. Passing through rows of brightly painted yellow wakemakers, he could hear the clamor of maintenance workers and riggers buzzing about like a swarm of bees, busily completing final preparations before being reassigned to the frontlines. Weaving through the maze of aircraft, Parker finally came upon the trainer he had been issued since his first day at Maver's, the same one he had flown nearly every day over the last sixty days. He reached up and ran his fingers along the underbelly of the cockpit. Closing his eyes, he reflected upon his achievement with an air of satisfaction. This feeling of contentment, however, was tinged by the weight of regret and emptiness he felt when he realized that he was celebrating alone. Parker wished somehow that he could share his happiness with those he loved, but the facts remained that both of his parents were gone, his sister was missing, and his wife was far away. Again, he began to doubt the seemingly impulsive decision that had led him to this moment. The urgent desire to find his sister was now tempered by a deep sense of longing for Tilly and a homesick heart. "Well, here I am," he thought to himself. "I hope I made the right choice." He looked up to the sky above. "Please, let it be right."

Parker felt a tap on his shoulder and turned to see whom it was. Standing before him was Rex, glowing bright red and reeking of alcohol.

"Here's to grinding it out and for keeping your thickey wicket!" With a big smile, Rex handed Parker a half-empty bottle of brill.

"Here's to both of us." Parker said as he lifted the bottle and guzzled down a healthy swig of the high-proof liquor.

"Yep, starting tomorrow, it's out of the can and into the pan," Rex slurred and flopped onto the ground.

Parker sat down next to him. "Any idea where we're headed?"

"Word has it we've been assigned intercept detail somewhere up north."

Parker took another gulp and handed the bottle back.

Rex puckered his lips as the savory mash burned a caustic trail down his gullet. "You know, I never thought I'd make it through. The fact is I've never finished anything in my life until now. Everyone in my town thought I was a washout. And who knows? Maybe they're right. But at least now they'll have to look up if they want to shoot old Rexy down."

"Cheers to that," Parker toasted.

"So, Parker, which of the three P's brought you out here? Pride? Patriotism? Or propaganda?"

Parker sighed. "A curse."

Rex looked puzzled. "Wait a minute. That doesn't start with a P." He searched through the catacombs of his inebriated mind and snapped his fingers. "Prophecy, now that's a P."

"Prophecy it is," Parker agreed.

With a final toss of the bottle, Rex concluded, "Well, here's to happy days and happy hunting." Wiping his mouth with the sleeve of his uniform, he belched. "Jiggers! Now, that's the capper."

Gradually, somberness weighed on the moment. Parker broke the silence by asking hesitantly, "Say Rex, are you scared?"

Ever jubilant, Rex shook his head. "Scared? Who? Me? Heck no. Why, it's gonna be a cakewalk. Besides, the way I see it, who'd want to shoot down a mutt like me? It doesn't make for much of a story. Kind of like kicking a three-legged dog or something."

Though his words said one thing, something in Rex's voice told a different story.

"Well, buddy, I better go check on my crate and make sure those oil cans fixed up the trim on my portside stabilizer. I'll catch you back in the racks."

"Right."

Rex stood up and teetered. Adjusting his cap, he saluted Parker before staggering away.

Parker placed his hands behind his head and leaned back onto the turf. The night was clear and the stars sparkled brightly. The glow of a full moon cast a reflection across the soft contours of the wakemaker's fuselage. He thought of Tilly back at home and wondered if she might also be dreaming of the day when they would be reunited.

Unbeknownst to Parker, Tilly was about to embark on her own journey. The secret left unrevealed to him was quickly becoming evident, as Tilly was four months closer to becoming a mother. Her bags packed and Smilie by her side, she stepped out of the hovel and into the night. She was off for a quick trip to a maternity ward located along the Haedyrn Plateau for a general checkup and to visit with the den mother, who had cared for her during her days at the orphanage.

A porter accompanied by a medical mech came to escort her down to the airfield.

Smilie, who was always excited to go for a walk, began barking at the moon.

"Okay, Smilie, calm down. I get it. It must be a full moon tonight. You always go crazy for them."

Tilly recalled the image she saw as a child before her accident – of the big bright disk that held the image of Leialilthethuthenang, "The Rabbit," positioned in the center. Even now, despite the scarring to the corneas of her eyes, there was no denying the contrast of the moon's glow against the black sky. "I wish you were here, Parker," she wondered out loud. "Maybe I should have told you, but would it have changed anything?"

"Excuse me, ma'am? Did you say something?" the porter asked.

"No, just mumbling to myself."

Guiding her up the entry, he advised, "Be careful on those steps, mum. They can be a bit tricky and we want to get you there in one piece."

"Thank you," Tilly replied.

As she entered the transport, she could feel the moonbeams connecting her with her husband. She took a seat next to a window and projected a final thought to her beloved: "Be safe."

It was early the next morning when the fog-laden tranquility at Maver's field was disturbed by a single turbine whirring to life. Soon another joined, then another. Eventually, there was a raucous cacophony of blasting air and roaring engines that could be heard miles away. With the new pilots having been assigned to their combat rotations, they were now all in the process of venturing off to join their awaiting squadrons.

In a minute, the base would be completely barren of pilots and aircraft. Some were heading south toward the Slewy Wetlands at Quick, while others like Parker and Rex headed to the highlands along the east coast of Squeller.

Excitement buzzed as both pilots and replacement crews scurried to board their ships. Parker hopped into his cockpit, harnessed in and began quickly running through his instrument checklist. He peered through the side windshield and saw Rex giving him a big thumbs-up as his pod ascended into the air. Parker waved back and gently pushed the vertical throttle lever to takeoff. The powerful hoverball located behind his cockpit rumbled to life and gently eased the ship upward. Once out of ground effect, Parker engaged the two counter-rotating propulsion fans and accelerated his wakemaker into a smooth climb.

Catching up with the others, he set coordinates into the auto-nav and leaned back to take in the grandeur of the open sky. The air was crisp and clear and despite the random buffet every now and then, the journey north was a truly relaxing affair.

As their destination approached, the group came in low over the white-capped sea. The cliffs of pale white sandstone and jagged outcrops proved an awe-inspiring sight as the squadron lined single file into landing formation and approached the rocky jetty that housed the underground base at Squeller.

Parker flipped on his landing lights as the sun-filled sky abruptly disappeared under a veil of darkness and his pod entered the mouth of an enormous cavern. At the far end of the tunnel, shafts of light streamed through the ceiling and sparkled off the tidal current that washed ashore along the tiered interior rotunda. The multi-leveled hangar docked twenty or so ships along a series of platforms that bridged out from the chiseled walkways and networked together like a skeletal jigsaw puzzle.

A voice crackled over Parker's intercom. "Trainer one-eight, attach at platform B, docking bay nine."

"Copy, Control, hook nine."

Parker hovered over an extended ramp and waited as a large metal claw clamped around the main stabilizer of his wakemaker and pulled him over a grated metal platform. Powering down the engines, he exited the cockpit and hopped down onto the landing pad. It felt good to be on solid ground again. Parker stretched his back and cracked the kinks out of his neck. He noticed Rex's pod docked just ahead and saw his friend, still hung-over, walking over to greet him.

"Well, here we are," said Rex. "All nestled nicely and packed in like a tin of greasy grayvel."

Parker scanned the enormity of the complex and asked Rex, "Have you ever seen anything like this before?"

"So what, it's big, but it ain't much for getting a tan," Rex replied cheekily. "Did I ever tell you that I'm afraid of the dark?"

Over a loudspeaker, an announcement echoed. "Flight crews report to lower level, Platform E." The voice repeated. "All flight crews report to lower level, Platform E."

"I guess that's us," Parker said.

"Lead the way," Rex ushered with a wave of his arm.

Through the maze of stairwells and corridors, Parker and Rex assembled with the other pilots and personnel on the bottom deck of the station near the edge of the waterfront. The fledgling group huddled close together and waited eagerly to see who would come to address them. Parker looked around and spotted a few individuals he recognized from training, while the rest, he assumed, must have transferred in from other squadrons or bases.

At the end of a pier, a large-framed man lighted a pipe with his back turned. By his stature alone, Parker knew it had to be Jumbo. The figure turned to face the crowd and released a puff of smoke from the corner of his pursed lips. He spotted Parker standing at the edge of the litter of rookie pilots and nodded a friendly greeting, but Parker turned away, pretending not to see him.

Though Jumbo thought it peculiar, he quickly turned his attention to addressing the assembly. "Welcome Group Three-Eight-Six," he began. "I'm Breaker Lien. I'm the Squadron Leader here and your CO during this rotation. I understand that some of you are re-o's from other units, blackballs and dodgers, while the rest of you are factory fresh and new whacks on the chopping block." He looked down to review his notes. "According to my records, Air Armory has assigned you the moniker, 'Button Blue Squadron.'"

A booming growl erupted in the background, interrupting Jumbo's speech. The group turned their attention to a damaged fighter sputtering in for an emergency landing. As the wakemaker crash-landed near the shore, the smoking engines ground to a halt. Parker looked on intensely as a nearby rigger helped a wounded pilot out of the cockpit. The pilot's arm was dangling and bloodied and his face was blackened with the soot from burning circuits. A medical crew rushed over with a gurney and quickly escorted the pilot away to the infirmary.

Jumbo sighed. "In case any of you are wondering, there goes the best shot in the house." He exhaled another puff of smoke and took a moment to gather his thoughts. "Reports say the Crinch have acquired total occupation over Downy. That means strikes will be coming in fast and furious. We're on our last legs out here and the game now is about survival. Coastal Air Intercept is positioned as the final stronghold against imminent invasion." He scanned the sea of wide eyes staring back at him. "The rules here are simple. Hit the enemy hard, sleep whenever you can, and most important of all, bring your crate back at all costs. We're losing fighters faster than we can recycle them. Be sure to check in with Aux and Intel to receive your kit and duty roster. Get some food and some rest, and try to settle in as best you can. That's it. Any questions?" The group stood silently. "No? Good. Welcome to Squeller." With a sharp nod, Jumbo dismissed the group and headed over to check on the condition of the injured pilot.

Upon receiving his welcome kit that included a set of thermal clothing, toiletries, ID patches, and a portfolio filled with maps, manuals, and other documents, pangs of hunger began to ache in Parker's belly. Alongside him, Rex's stomach made a grumbling moan, as neither of them had eaten since morning.

Rex pulled the map from under Parker's nose and tossed it into a bin. "Forget that, buddy. We've got all night to flip through that junk. I don't know about you, but I'm starving." He scratched his head and looked around for a directory. "So, where do you think they keep the local feed trough?"

"Beats me," Parker said. "But it's probably listed somewhere on that map you just threw away."

"Oh, Parker, you don't need a stinking map to find food. Just follow your nose." And like a trusted hound, Rex sniffed his way back into the complex on a mission to find a kitchen.

Their stomachs full and bodies refreshed with a hot shower and shave, Parker and Rex jovially approached the open hangar to find their pods reconfigured for combat. Heavy stabilizers with large-caliber pressure cannons were now installed along the hard-points, giving the trusty fighters a robust and durable profile. The upper halves of the fuselage and canopy were now painted blue with the ventral side camouflaged in a light gray. The swift and gentle contours of the old trainer had now been transformed into a rugged machine of war.

Parker cautiously approached his wakemaker. He could sense a fearsome aura exuding from the heavy guns. Feeling uneasy, he turned to Rex and asked. "So, what do you think it's like, being at the other end of a barrel?"

Rex shrugged, "I don't know. And I'm not planning on finding out. I figure it's a lot like gettin' kicked in the crotch, memorable but not all that much fun. But we won't have to worry about that 'cause we're going to be too busy chalking up marks and grinning like the mice that stole the cheese. Right?"

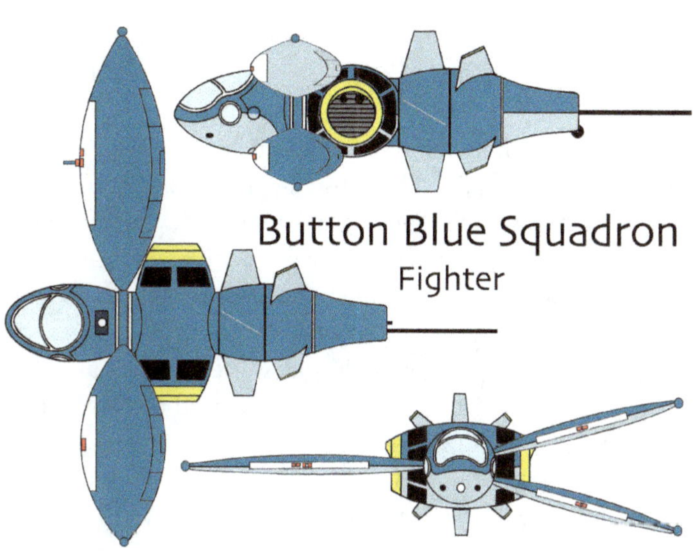

"Right," Parker nodded at Rex's lighthcarted, if not overly optimistic, prediction. He felt fortunate to have a friend who possessed such a relaxed disposition to keep him from becoming overly anxious.

Rex smiled, "Chin up, buddy. Like I told you before, it's gonna be a cakewalk." He stretched his arms and yawned. "Now, I don't know about you, but I'm just about ready to fall flat on my face."

"It's been a long day," Parker agreed. "I guess we should pack it in?"

"I'll see you in the morning,"

Rex entered his cubby and the light inside dimmed. Standing alone at the end of the platform, Parker tried desperately to calm his troubled mind. He gazed upon the docked wakemaker somberly, like a family member might view a corpse. The exhilaration and romance of the previous months were now only a distant memory, as the fear of uncertainty that once plagued Parker's thoughts had suddenly returned. Fortunately for him, a deep wave of exhaustion washed over his body and helped to calm his nerves. He turned away from the railing and walked over to his quarters.

He tapped on an illuminated switch with his surname stenciled underneath. The frosted-glass door slid open to reveal a small rectangular dugout. Only a few meters wide, the stark room felt strangely large and empty. The floors were made of concrete and the unfinished walls were roughly chiseled and grainy to the touch. Its modular design was efficiently arranged with a simple storage bunk, an open wardrobe, a desk, and a chair. This hollowed-out box was to be his home away from home for the next several months and made him feel more like a prisoner than a pilot.

Taking a seat on the bedside, Parker removed his boots and jacket. Then, leaning back onto the thin mattress, he stretched out his arms and legs. Surprisingly, the "sled" with only a thin layer of cushioning felt amazingly comfortable. Maybe it was just in his mind, but it felt really good to lay prone and extended. With a slide of a rheostat, Parker dimmed the lights to a point where he could just see the soft silhouette of the wakemaker through the translucent glass. He placed his hands behind his head and stared upward at the ceiling. Gradually, his eyes became heavy as he fell into a peaceful slumber.

RING! RING! The alarm bell dinned. Startled but still half-asleep, Parker needed a moment to figure out where he was and what was going on. The door to his cubby slid open and he saw Rex waving exuberantly at him.

"Wake up, Parker! This is it!"

In a flash, he threw off the covers and hopped out of bed. Stumbling, he did his best to strap on his boots and gather his jacket and flight gear as he scurried out the door.

Along the crowded walkway, Parker found the hangar to be a flurry of commotion. Pilots were seen boarding their fighters as riggers finished last-minute checks on their handiwork. Parker hopped into his cockpit and engaged the turbines to begin pressurizing the pod. With deft skill, he flipped switches and turned knobs in preparation for takeoff. Then with a pat on his flight helmet, he adjusted the microphone against his lips.

Rex's voice blared out through his radio headset. "Parker, you prepped?"

"Yeah, she's coming around."

The hydraulic docking clamp detached from the fighter, and it wavered gently before settling into a stable hover. Parker pushed the throttle forward and listened as the propellers began to buzz. Within a matter of seconds, his wakemaker was swiftly accelerating out of the hangar and into the clear morning sky.

High amongst the clouds, the squadron assembled into formation. There were six fighters aligned in a boomerang-shaped formation. Jumbo was at the lead, with Parker and the graduating class's top protégé Merv set close along his wing tips. Following along the starboard side were the remaining three rookies: Rex, Windal, and the squadron's tail ender, a lanky flyer named Skink.

A message from Air Armory fizzled in over the intercom. "Button Blue Leader, this is Peek-A-Boo. Contact seven specters at flight level three-zero, grid two-eight-eight."

Jumbo repeated the coordinates and surveyed the area. He spotted a formation of heavy bombers trailing lines of dark gray smoke and being escorted by a pair of Crinch fighters.

"Copy Peek-A-Boo, targets acquired." Jumbo adjusted the pressure in his weapons and announced to the squadron, "All right, this is it. We'll hit in two waves. Button Four take your flight and separate the fighters. Two and Three, you're with me. Make sure to dive in with your throttles wide open; otherwise, you'll bleed off and get tagged on the way out."

The squadron broke up into two groups as instructed, with the first flight led by Jumbo swooping in for an attack on the bombers. Parker braced for the battle and accelerated the pod up to attack speed. When the enemy aircraft veered into view, butterflies rustled nervously in his stomach.

Merv, on the contrary, was eager and ready to rumble. His eyes widened and he began salivating like a hungry dog waiting for a meal. Licking his lips, he could feel his trigger finger getting twitchy. Suddenly, a strong vibration began rattling in his secondary turbine. He pushed and pulled the throttle lever but received no response. He called out over the intercom, "Button Leader, this is Button Three. There's a knock in my can and I'm losing pressure. I can't keep up."

"Copy that, Button Three. Angle out and return to base."

Frustrated, Merv muttered, "Stinking junk spinner."

"Lucky duck," Parker whispered under his breath, wishing that he, too, could be going home.

With the bombers now in firing range, Jumbo positioned in for the kill. "There they are. Button Two, hit the trailer on the left, I've got the right. Angle in and give 'em a quick squirt."

"Co-copy, Leader," Parker stuttered nervously.

Jumbo locked the bomber in his sights and squeezed the trigger. The cannons popped in quick succession and a trail of tracer fire streamed across the ship's midsection. Bits of paneling plinked from the fuselage until a massive explosion from the bomb bay caused the craft to disintegrate into a fiery cloud.

"That's one!" Jumbo shouted victoriously through the intercom. From the corner of his eye, he spotted Parker's pod beginning to veer away.

"Get in there, Parker! Take the shot!"

Parker's heart raced as the enemy bomber filled his target reticule, but a surge of panic made it impossible for him to pull the trigger. Parker could feel the cold hand of death resting on his shoulder. His fingers were numb and his hands were shaking like leaves blowing in the wind.

Jumbo's voice pierced through the headsets as he ordered, "Button Two, you've got the angle. Take the shot!"

Parker's finger slid from the trigger and he could hear the clink of the metal guard as it closed over the control stick.

"Take the shot!" Jumbo shouted a final time.

"No, it's no good," Parker replied timidly.

Jumbo was livid. "What are you talking about? It doesn't get any better than that!"

Frightened, Parker angled his fighter away from the battle.

Jumbo struck the side of the canopy with the palm of his hand and broke away from pursuit of the bombers to rally with his insubordinate wingman.

A few miles back, Rex and the others were busily wrangling in a dogfight with the enemy escorts. The last member of the group, Skink, was in an especially bad way. Blasted by a heavy dose of Crinch hospitality, the greenhorn pilot struggled to shake off the attack.

He shouted into the microphone, "Someone get over here and get this flicker off me!"

Having spotted Skink's wakemaker diving evasively, Windal rolled in to lend a hand. "Hang in there, Skink! I'm on it!" He squinted with determination as his ship swooped in behind the enemy and fired a burst that narrowly missed the nimble fighter.

More rounds shattered the propeller blades off of Skink's spinner and punched holes through his secondary turbine. A stream of pressurized gas spewed from the pod as it began to crumble. Panic-stricken, Skink shrieked, "She's gonna blow!"

Unable to get a clean shot, Windal shouted over the intercom, "Punch out, Skink! Eject!!"

The battered wakemaker folded in a shower of twisted metal that blazed a stream of debris across the sky.

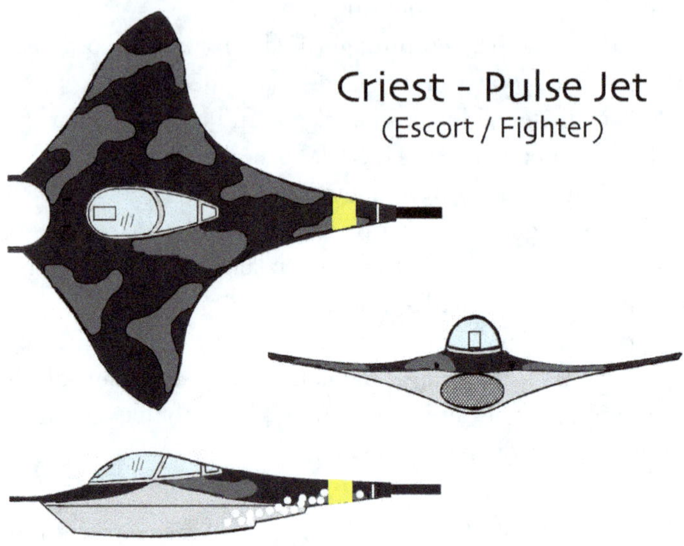

Windal pulled up to avoid the wreckage but soon found himself falling prey to the second Crinch fighter. Bullets ricocheted throughout his cockpit, splattering blood across the windshield. He grimaced in pain and looked down to see the fingers of his stick hand dangling like twigs inside a mangled glove. Reaching over with his other hand, he tried his best to steady the pod that was quickly losing altitude. Knowing the enemy had him dead to rights, Windal accepted his fate and shut his eyes.

"Mother, make it quick," he prayed.

A loud explosion erupted from behind.

From over the intercom, a cheerful voice rang out, "Bingo!"

Windal peeked his eyes open and caught sight of Rex's wakemaker sliding up alongside.

"Stamp that Ruddy on my tubby. You all right there, Winnie?"

"Well, there goes my penmanship," Windal exhaled in relief. "My parent's are going to be furious."

"Don't worry, we'll have you scribbling that pigeon scratch of yours in no time. Until then, level out and stay close."

"Right behind you," Windal confirmed, happy to be alive.

As the remaining bombers dispersed, Jumbo set up for a final attack. He pushed up alongside Parker's pod and eyeballed him through the windshield.

"Button Two, form up. Stay high off my port beam and give me cover. You got that?"

"Copy, Leader." Parker replied as he fell back to provide protection.

As they angled in on a trailing bomber, a final enemy escort dove in from above and opened fire.

"Jumbo, I've got one on my tail!"

Jumbo adjusted his attitude. "I've got the buzzard in my sights. Just hold him off for a few more seconds."

A trail of tracer fire beamed ahead of Parker's cockpit.

"I can't! He's got me beat!"

"Hang in there, Button Two!" Jumbo ordered. He lined the bomber into view and squeezed the trigger. Bits trickled from the bomber's wing, but he missed the main engines that were at the heart of the beast. Jumbo reduced his speed and edged in for another shot. "Come on, baby. Angle up."

A second barrage of cannon fire blazed past Parker's pod. This time he could hear the dull plinking of damage being scored across his tail. "He's got me locked!"

"Sit tight," Jumbo instructed Parker. "I've almost got him!"

"I can't!"

Terrified, Parker pulled the ejection lever located alongside his seat. A series of explosive bolts cast away the cockpit's forward windshield, followed by a pneumatic blast that sent him hurling upward into the open sky.

"Damn it!" Jumbo squeezed one last failed attempt on the bomber before rolling away. He watched in disgust as the enemy bomber fled the battle and disappeared in the clouds. Jumbo caught sight of Parker's chute fluttering below. He banged his head against the back of the chair before regrouping with the rest of the squadron.

Curtly, he demanded an update. "All right, everyone, give me a count."

"Button Four, clear," Rex responded.

"Five clear," Windal followed.

Rex spotted Parker's parachute. "I think I see a chute on two."

"Concur," Jumbo sneered. "Mark the grid and tag a rover for pickup. Any of you seen Skink?"

"He's in the drink," Rex replied.

"Copy that," Jumbo grumbled. "Level out and head back to base."

Staggering back into formation, the remaining units of Button Blue vectored a course back to Squeller.

Drifting down along the shoreline near the Sandilarn Cliffs, Parker thudded onto the soft beach. He rushed to collect his parachute and felt his heart pounding with adrenaline and his nerves frayed and splintered. He fiddled with the homing beacon attached to his inflatable bobber and pulled the emergency pin. Once the signal began to pulse, he unfastened the straps on the life preserver and pulled it off over his head. Parker then folded the inflatable vest into a makeshift pillow and placed it on the ground.

Exhausted, he collapsed onto the sandy shore and closed his eyes. Terror from his brush with death left him feeling fragile and ashamed. "What am I doing here?" he asked himself. "I'm no fighter pilot, I'm too damn scared." His emotions felt raw and his mind was tangled in a web of fear and confusion. His eyes burst open and he cried out to the spirits above, "Please, I don't want to die! I don't want to die!!!"

In the shortened daylight hours of winter, it was dark by the time Parker arrived back to base. The rescue transport docked at an umbilical located near the infirmary where Rex stood with a big smile waiting to greet him. The twin hydraulic doors swung open and Parker exited the ship with his chute tucked under his arm.

Rex pointed at the tuft of ruffled synthetic silk and said, "So that bag of yarn actually works."

Parker quietly dumped the chute into a recycle bin for cleaning and repacking.

"We missed you this afternoon." Rex continued, "There was another attack at Keller near the Cove. Jumbo shot down two more, which makes three kills in one day. Three! Can you believe that?"

"Sounds like a real barrel of fun," Parker said bitterly.

"Lucky bastard! That guy gets all the prime shots," Rex smirked.

"Well, it's good to be the king."

"Ain't that the truth?"

Sensing Parker's resentment, Rex tempered his enthusiasm and patted him on the shoulder. "Well, I for one am glad to have you back. You really had me worried."

Parker felt guilty for snapping at Rex and politely replied, "Thanks. I just wish I was happy to be back."

"Look, why don't you go check in? We can catch up later on deck. In the meantime, I'll go find us a little liquid relaxation."

"I could use a drink." Parker nodded before turning to leave.

Rex snapped his fingers, "Hold on, Park. I almost forgot. The CO wants to see you. He's waiting over in briefing."

"Great," Parker sighed. "Time to pay the piper."

Through the open doorway, Parker saw Jumbo leaning against the center podium enjoying a puff on his familiar pipe. Violence ruled his thoughts when he saw Jumbo, his "old friend," enjoying the soothing aroma of fragrant smoke while those he commanded were off suffering in the infirmary or, worse, blasted apart and cast to the hereafter in the skies above. As his resentment grew, Parker's hand unconsciously curled into a fist.

Unaware, Jumbo sucked in a long drag from the glowing embers before turning to face his wingman. A smashing left hook across the jaw met his greeting and caused the smoldering pipe to slip from his lips. Instantly, Jumbo caught the pipe before it hit the floor. He calmly straightened his posture and cracked his neck. Without saying a word, he slowly exhaled a lungful of smoke.

"Do you feel better?"

"No," Parker seethed.

"Good," Jumbo remarked before placing the pipe back in his mouth. "I could have you sent to the brig for that, but I'll let that one go since I know you had a tough first day."

"Tough?" Parker snapped. "You left me hanging out to dry!"

Jumbo mumbled out the side of his mouth, "That's your job."

"It's my job to end up as fodder to your glory chasing?"

"We all put it on the line, Parker."

"Yeah, only, some of us are given a very thin rope."

Jumbo rebutted, "Look, if you would have hit that bloody flicker when you had the chance, I wouldn't have had to go back for seconds."

"You're sick, Jumbo. You know that? You're a bloody maniac!"

"And you're a spineless coward," Jumbo said bluntly. "Kiki was wrong about you."

Parker's fury erupted again and he slugged Jumbo across the face, this time sending the pipe flying across the room.

In an amazing display of self-control, Jumbo kept his composure and slowly lifted two fingers. "That's two. The next one's going to cost you," he said, massaging his jaw. "I know you blame me for her death, but I assure you I did everything possible to keep her safe."

"Oh, is that so? Well, you must have done a pretty poor job, because I don't see her here."

"It's called war, Parker. People die."

"She's not dead!" Parker shouted back.

"Not dead? What are you talking about? I was there when she went down."

"No!" Parker vehemently denied. "You're wrong. She's alive!"

"What are you, some kind of a nut? Why can't you get it through that thick skull of yours that she's gone?" He edged in closer. "Kaput, finito… She ain't coming back."

His eyes burning with rage, Parker lunged wildly at Jumbo in a tantrum. He punched as hard as he could and pressed with great ferocity, but his anger kept him unbalanced and ineffective against the hardened combat mettle of Jumbo, who previously had served as an infantry specialist. Jumbo allowed Parker to expel his wrath before striking back. Having taken enough abuse, Jumbo thrust a mighty blow straight into Parker's belly. The impact sent Parker crashing to the floor and gasping for air. Bloodied and bruised, Jumbo limped his way to the corner of the room and reached down for his still smoldering pipe. He took a couple of light puffs before taking a seat next to Parker.

"Parker, what are you doing here?" he asked, "This ain't your party."

"I'm here because of you," Parker groaned. "It's your fault. You were supposed to watch out for her."

"Kiki and I both made our choice."

"I trusted you."

"Look, you can blame me all you like, but it isn't going to bring her back."

"It wasn't her fight!"

"It's everyone's fight."

"No, not hers!"

"Yes, hers, too!" Jumbo leaned his head back against the wall and sighed. "I wish I could bring her back. I wish I could bring them all back." He tapped the edge of his pipe on the ground and began cleaning the bowl with his finger. "Maybe you don't know what goes on out here, but I've seen so many people die that I can't remember their names anymore. I can only see their faces staring back at me during the night. You think you're the only one suffering? I've got a dozen ghosts haunting my dreams and I spend the rest of my waking hours waiting for cherries like you to get pitted in the press." Jumbo blew a puff of air into the pipe's bowl and slipped it back into his pocket. "I loved her," he said sadly.

"Probably more than you'd care to believe. But she's gone now and I've learned to accept that. And you better do the same. That is, if you plan on staying alive."

Parker shook his head defiantly.

"I'm giving it to you straight, Parker. You've got skills and you're smart. Almost everything I want in a pilot. But you're scared and that makes you a liability. I know you live with firm conviction and that deep down you're a strong person. I've seen it firsthand and I'm feeling a little bit of it right now," he grinned as he licked the blood oozing from the corner of his mouth. "But I won't hold your hand, and I don't have the time or the resources to allow you to ditch every time we go up. If you're not ready for the sickle, don't tempt the reaper." Standing up, Jumbo buttoned his collar back into place and exited the hall with a final remark. "It's your choice."

Parker sat quietly, slumped, alone and confused. He thought to himself, "Jumbo's right. I am a coward. Too scared to die and even more afraid to live." Stuck between a rock and a hard place, Parker felt the weight of the world on his shoulders. Jumbo had spelled it out, simple and clear, and it was now up to him to decide what to do next.

The next morning, Parker emerged from his cubby, refreshed by the first full night of sleep he had since transferring to Squeller. The sleep did wonders in helping to clear his mind. He stepped out onto the catwalk and noticed Rex meticulously stenciling a kill marker onto the side of his cockpit.

Walking over to the edge of the dock, he watched as Rex carefully examined his handiwork.

"So, what do you think?" Rex asked.

"Very nice."

"It's only half a kill. I credited the other half to Skink. I figure it's the least I could do."

Parker nodded in agreement.

"So how'd it go last night? Did he crack the whip?"

"Does it show?"

"A little."

Rex leaned back on his elbows and reflected upon his first victory. "Beautiful. Absolutely beautiful," he chirped with an air of satisfaction. "If only those daft buggers back at home could see me now, boy, I'd show them. And with any luck, I'll string up a nice row before spring."

Parker fidgeted uneasily.

Emotionally, the two were on opposite ends of the spectrum. It was only when Rex caught sight of Parker's empty umbilical that he finally realized the error in his boasting. An uneasy silence grew between the two friends. After a while, Parker finally broke the tension and asked, "Rex, what am I doing here?"

"The same thing we're all doing here: killing time and killing Crinch."

"When we left Maver's, did you think it was going to be like this?"

Rex shrugged. "Sure… Well, sort of… I don't know. I guess it's a little rougher than I thought." He scanned the trail of recently patched holes along the side of his wakemaker's fuselage. "It's funny. Before I got here, I was all ready to hop in and start rippin' tail. But after yesterday, I'm not so sure. For some reason, I've got a strange feeling we're the ones drawing the short straw."

Parker took a seat next to Rex and confessed. "I don't know what happened yesterday. All I remember was being scared out of my wits. I couldn't move. I couldn't breathe. All I wanted to do was bail the hell out."

Rex tried to encourage him. "Look, there's no shame in tossing the kite. You were taking hits. I would have done the same."

"No, you wouldn't."

"I'm serious, I would. It's no joke up there. They're playing for keeps and we're no good to Air Armory dead."

"Well, you, they can use. But as for me, I'm just taking up space. Jumbo was right. I don't belong here."

"Hey, steady. It's just the funk, Parker. We all had it."

"Sure, but none of you bailed out."

"And not all of us came back, either. It's okay to be scared, buddy. You'll swat 'em good next time."

"Next time? Maybe you haven't noticed, but I'm halfway out the door."

"Don't sweat it. You'll get another chance, you'll see. The CO's a good guy."

"Well, I doubt if –"

RING!!! The alarm bell signaled an oncoming attack. Rex leaped up from the deck and buckled into his parachute.

"Dust a little pepper for me," Parker encouraged.

"Don't worry, I'll season 'em good!"

From below, Parker heard a whistle. He looked down and saw Jumbo waving at him. "Are you in?"

Parker pointed at his empty umbilical and answered. "No pod!"

Jumbo glanced across the hangar and caught sight of Windal's unoccupied wakemaker docked across the way. He signaled to Parker, "Down here, take five!"

"See, I told you," Rex grinned.

Parker nodded half-heartedly. The doubt that had plagued his thoughts earlier turned into nervous anticipation as he scrambled to gather his flight gear.

On the deck below, Jumbo did a quick pre-flight check on his wakemaker's battle-damaged undercarriage while his trusted mechanic, Socket, rushed frantically to complete a last-minute repair.

"Is she ready to dance?" Jumbo asked.

"Sir, I don't think this bucket of bolts is going to hold together. I've still got holes from last week left to plug, not to mention the spar fatigue I detected along the starboard stabilizer. I don't think it's such a good idea."

"She's a tough old bird. She'll manage." Jumbo slapped the main fuselage and a small panel dropped onto the platform. Picking up the metal card, he hopped into the cockpit. As he secured himself into position, he handed the plate over to the mechanic. "Must be extra."

Socket made a final plea. "Sir, I really think you should reconsider. At least give me a couple of days to replace the secondary. I don't know how much more stress it can take."

"Well, there's only one way to find out. Don't worry. When I get back, you can give her a proper shakedown."

Jumbo engaged the engines and sealed the canopy. A blast of compressed air shot from the blower's turbine and blew the mechanic back. Once up to full power, Jumbo disengaged from the docking umbilical and headed toward the exit.

Across the way, Parker rushed down the catwalk and over to Windal's fighter, where a young rigger was wiping down the forward windshield. Stepping up onto the main stabilizer, Parker snapped on a chute and asked, "Will it fly?"

"She's charged. But I wouldn't –"

Parker gripped the control stick and noticed remnants of dry blood and bones splattered across the instrument panel and canopy.

"I'm sorry about that, sir," the rigger apologized. "I didn't think anyone would be taking her out today. I barely had enough time to get the mechanics in order."

Parker closed his eyes and took a deep breath to settle his nerves. Once the initial shock had passed, he looked back at the young man and exhaled. "That's all right. Adds a bit of color." He extended a hand. "Name's Parker."

"Paddock, sir."

"Nice to meet you."

The two shook hands.

Parker pulled down the padded horse collar and pointed up to the level above. "If I make it back, I'll be parking her topside."

"Right, sir. Happy hunting."

Paddock stepped back from the umbilical and waved as the wakemaker's forward windshield lowered into place. Parker adjusted the manifold pressure and prepped the engines for takeoff. With a push of a button, the mighty turbines whirred to life and he quickly sped from the hangar to group with the others.

Catching up with the squadron, Parker aligned into formation. Over the radio, orders broadcast in from Fighter Command. "Button Blue Squadron, contact four specters at flight level four-zero, grid two-nine-six, heading south-southwest at one-nine-five."

"Copy, Peek-A-Boo," Jumbo acknowledged. "Grid two-ninety six." He checked both sides and did a quick count on the formation. "All right, you heard the man. Let's get in there." With a push on the throttle, Jumbo accelerated his wakemaker up to attack speed.

Rex was the first to catch sight of the enemy and called out over the intercom, "Contact three bombers two o'clock low. Looks like heavies."

Jumbo scanned the skies above for signs of an escort. Not having seen any, he ordered, "Stay sharp and keep an eye open for fighters hiding in the sun."

Merv spotted the accompanying escort, "Contact! Two specters, ten o'clock high!"

"I see them," Jumbo concurred. "Three and four break off and intercept the fighters. Five, you're with me."

"Copy, leader," Rex confirmed.

The squadron broke up into two pairs, with one going high and the other low.

"Stay tight, Parker," Jumbo ordered. "And don't squeeze until you're all the way in, got it?"

"Check."

A malfunction indicator flashed on Parker's instrument display and the crosshairs on his illuminated targeting sight disappeared. Parker radioed, "Jumbo, I just lost my scope!"

"Just ease in and take your best shot."

As the bombers lined up into view, a loud jolt violently rocked Jumbo as the leading edge of the main stabilizer tore from the wing of his pod. The flight controls felt sluggish and maintaining control over the ship was becoming difficult. This, however, was the least of his worries as a shower of bullets hailed in from above. Jumbo shouted over the intercom, "Someone get down here and bounce this buzzard off me!"

Rex angled in pursuit. "Hang on, leader. We're on it."

More rounds ripped through Jumbo's turbines, and he began to lose pressure. "Jiggers! She's coming apart!" He wrestled desperately to keep the wakemaker flying. "Parker, I can't keep up. Get in there and blast 'em!"

Parker acknowledged as Jumbo disengaged from the fight and headed for home.

Beams of tracer fire streamed in ahead as well as from behind and Parker could see tiny flashes of machine gun fire twinkling out from the tail end of the bombers. Caught in the crossfire, he called for help. "Rex, I'm in trouble!"

"I'm almost there!" Rex responded.

Parker's wakemaker rattled as a line of bullets splattered across his front windshield and though he wanted desperately to flee, his body was frozen. Time slowed and everything became vivid and clear. He shut his eyes and grimaced. "This is it," he said, as another line of bullets plinked across the fuselage. Bracing for the end, he heard a thunderous explosion echo from behind his cockpit. In a flash, he recalled the long summer days back in Kakydurn, of being a child at play, and working as a radioman. He thought regretfully of Tilly and the happy life he abandoned.

As he waited for his inevitable demise, the sound of the blast faded and Parker heard a familiar voice bursting over the intercom, "Kaboom!"

Parker peeked open his eyes and, to his amazement, realized he was still in one piece.

Rex exclaimed jubilantly, "All right, pal. That cat's off your back! Now get in there and give 'em hell!"

Parker saw that the tail of the enemy's lead bomber filling his vision. Fumbling with the trigger guard, he managed to squeeze off a quick shot just in time. The mighty cannons burst to life, spewing dozens of metal darts into the bomber's backbone. Bits of paneling chipped off the dorsal armor until a single lucky round found its mark. The densely packed bomb bay detonated and engulfed the Crinch bomber in a brilliant fireball. The massive explosion sent a shower of shrapnel hurling into the engines of the other and sent both aircraft tumbling down in a trail of black smoke.

Parker watched in utter disbelief as the whole event unfolded before him. Fortune was truly on his side, for in a moment of unforeseen irony it was he who was now two kills closer to becoming an ace.

Over the headsets, he heard Rex cheering with excitement, "Hot dog!"

Parker felt a wave of euphoria wash over him. He pulled back on the control stick and rolled his fighter triumphantly before forming up with the rest of the squadron.

Rex smiled as Parker pulled up alongside and signaled a thumbs-up, "Way to go, shooter!"

Over the radio, Merv reported in. "Button Four, I lost the other bomber in the clouds and the escorts are scuttling. Looks like we're clear."

"Copy that," Rex concurred.

It was a good day for Button Blue Squadron: three kills with no losses.

Exhilaration electrified Parker. He felt liberated, having survived the deadly initiation of finally being confirmed as a combat pilot, but most of all, he felt lucky. Parker never fancied himself a lucky person. In fact, most of his life he believed he was downright doomed. But today was different. Today the good graces were with him. He had savored the sweet taste of victory and for the first time in his life felt the joy of truly being alive.

Back at Squeller, the fighters clamped back onto their respective docks. Still glowing from the successful sortie, Rex rushed over to congratulate Parker, who was resting in his pilot's chair, drenched in sweat. He waited patiently as the forward windshield opened and Parker lifted up his harness. With an enthusiastic tug, Rex hoisted Parker out of the cockpit and clamored, "You sure gave them a wallop! I mean, you really handed it to them."

"Thanks to you," Parker smiled.

As the mutual admiration continued, Parker noticed a blotch of red soaking through Rex's uniform. "Rex, you're bleeding!"

"Just a little love bite from one of those Crinch buzzards."

"You better have the M.O. take a look at that."

"It's nothing," Rex said unconcerned. That sentiment, however, changed when he felt the blood dripping from his fingertips and started to feel queasy. "On second thought, maybe you're right. The sight of blood always makes me turn green. Especially when it's mine." Shaking his head in disbelief, he said, "I still can't believe it! One shot. One perfect bloody shot."

From up the ramp, Merv shouted, "Helleva scrap, Parker! A double top!"

"Just lucky," Parker grinned.

"I wish I could be that lucky," Merv said. "I still haven't swiped a single scratch."

Rex patted Merv on the shoulder, "Well, old boy, what's there to say? Some of us got it, and some of us don't."

"Twin marks each. Dirty sods," Merv grumbled enviously.

"You know, this calls for a celebration," Rex declared. "Good times are hard to come by around these parts and I think I've got just the bottle for the occasion. Meet me here after debriefing. I'm going to get stitched up."

"Make it quick, I'm thirsty." Merv said licking his lips.

"I'll be back in a flash." He turned to Parker and grinned. "Now, aren't you glad you stuck around?"

Parker shrugged humbly as Rex covered the wound with his hand and made a brisk walk for the infirmary.

Merv said to Parker. "Oh, by the way. The CO wants to see you."

"Again? Did he look angry?" Parker asked.

"No, but he didn't look happy."

Parker acknowledged and swept off his flight helmet.

Merv congratulated Parker a final time before turning to leave. "One for the books, Park, a real banger. Let's hurry up and check in, then really wet our whiskers."

Parker nodded in agreement as he made his way over to a nearby lift and descended.

Down on the maintenance level, Parker searched for Jumbo's cubby. He snaked his way through a series of long corridors and began to wonder why Jumbo needed to meet with him privately.

He thought, "What could it be this time? Maybe he heard about the mission? Or maybe I should have run better cover. Does he blame me for his pod falling apart? And why the hell are his quarters located down here in the pits?"

By the time Parker spotted Jumbo leaning against a doorway, he was an emotional wreck.

"You wanted to see me?" he asked nervously.

Jumbo slowly exhaled a long stream of smoke. "I heard about the scrap today. Nice work."

"Thanks," Parker said relieved.

Jumbo tapped his pipe against a hand railing and slipped it back into his shirt pocket; his expression was grim. Parker knew something was amiss and braced himself for what was about to come.

"I called you here because I just received some bad news from home."

"What news?"

Jumbo did not mince words. "Kakkie was hit this morning. Carpeted with rotting gas."

Parker heart sank. "Bombed? How bad?"

"Reports show high casualty with eighty percent DOD. The Crinch have engaged in an all-out strike over the Midland sectors. Tac thinks they're trying to mow a direct path from the flats through the foothills and all the way through to March. It's an attempt to break the EDN and bust a line to the capital. If they can clear a route, they'll be able to split the country in two."

Jumbo went on with the details, but Parker was no longer listening. All he could think of was the home he loved and the wife he had left behind.

Jumbo continued, "There's no comm service out there, and from the preliminaries it looks pretty bad."

Parker stood motionless.

Jumbo knew it would be difficult for Parker to accept so he tried his best to ease his conscience, "There's nothing we could have done. They were out of range, not to mention the sheer number of ships we'd be up against."

Parker mind was in turmoil as he imagined the horrible atrocity that had befallen his last idyllic symbol of tranquility.

Jumbo tapped him on the shoulder. "Hey, Park? You there?"

Receiving no reaction, Jumbo snapped his fingers in front of Parker's eyes, "You listening? Wake up!"

Parker turned to face him, his eyes welling with tears. Terrified, he roared at the top of his lungs, "Tilly!!!"

Sweeping Jumbo aside, Parker dashed over to a wakemaker being serviced. He yanked off the charging cables and moorings and pushed past the attending crewman.

"Sir, this isn't your ship," the rigger pleaded.

But Parker heard nothing. He engaged the turbines and powered them up.

Jumbo signaled him to stop, "It's too late, Parker! Shut it down!"

Consumed by an overwhelming urge to save his wife and his home, Parker detached from the umbilical and thrust the throttle forward. The blast from the turbine blew over carts full of tools and equipment. The rigger grabbed hold of a railing, and even Jumbo had to crouch for cover against the powerful force produced by the ship's blower. The two looked on as the hijacked fighter sped from the hangar and disappeared out of sight.

It was afternoon when Parker arrived at Kakydurn. Landing on the outskirts of the village, he disembarked and stepped onto the slushy ground. The heavy acrid smell of incendiary bombs and rotting gas filled the cool humid air. The once vibrant community of floral pastures and subterranean hovels was now nothing more than a blackened wasteland. Craters of enormous size dotted the landscape as streams of caustic smoke floated like clouds of death blanketing the sky.

He rushed down to the main trail that led toward his childhood home. A dark foreboding permeated his thoughts. He desperately wanted to find Tilly safe and uninjured, but the vast devastation indicated otherwise. When he reached the hovel, Parker found the entry door crumbled and unhinged. Stepping over the broken timber, he entered the wrecked dwelling. Ceiling rafters lay collapsed on the living room floor, and rubble filled the area that was once the kitchen. For the second time in its history, the Harker hovel had been destroyed.

Parker made his way to the bedroom, calling his wife's name. "Tilly?"

Shuffling through the debris, he came across an old utility vest with her name embroidered across the chest pocket. He reached over and clung to it with both hands.

"Where are you?"

From outside, he heard footsteps approaching.

A glimmer of hope sparked. Could it be?

Parker jumped to his feet and scurried back to the entry. He exited the front door and spotted an old man in tattered clothing walking aimlessly up the trail.

He rushed over and grabbed the man by the shoulders. "Please, sir. Can you help me?" Parker pleaded. "I'm looking for my wife." He pointed at the hovel. "We lived over there. Have you seen her?"

The man did not respond, his gaze hollow and empty.

"Please! It's very important! A young lady with a dog, her name is Tilly."

Shell-shocked, the man uttered, "No one lives here anymore."

"Where did they go? Where is everyone?"

The old man pointed toward a distant horizon billowing smoke and ash. Parker released his grip and ran over toward the smoldering blaze.

The pungent aroma of corpses was undeniable, and Parker had to cover his nose to keep from vomiting.

Scrambling to the top of the ridge, he stood above the valley and surveyed the scene below. What he saw, he could not fully comprehend. A mass grave filled with hundreds of bodies lay strewn in a row. Dozens of mechs scurried about, sorting through the remains and preparing the dead for burial.

Parker shivered at the terrible sight and felt as if he was on the verge of a nervous breakdown. His knees buckled, and he dropped to the ground. He could no longer contain the grief that erupted from within, and he burst out screaming.

But no amount of shouting could protect him from the truth. He buried his head into the muddy soil and sobbed. He cried for Tilly, Smilie, his parents, and Kiki. He cried for his neighbors and his friends. But above all, he cried for himself. Filled with desperation and self-pity, his mind was pulled into a deep abyss.

Eventually, the tears ceased, and for some unknown reason, his spirit felt purged, numb of all feelings. All that remained was the void left behind of a life that once was. The burning wick of desire had been extinguished. War had broken him. He raised from the ground a changed man, shielded from pain but no longer feeling human.

In the distance, Old Gurdy stood witness, unwavering and still. Parker thought it ironic that this lone tree was one of the few things that survived the attack, and in a strange way felt connected to it, as if they were both orphans of a lost history. He made his way over and patted the gnarled trunk with his hand. "Hey, old girl. It's nice to see you." He took a familiar seat at the base of the truck and huddled his knees close to his chest. The canopy of leaves rustled lightly and surrounded him in a gentle cloak. Parker closed his eyes and recalled the happier days spent relaxing under the protection of the old oak tree.

So much had happened that it was mind-boggling to think only a few hours earlier he was dueling in the skies above and face to face with his own mortality. But somehow fate had dealt him a different hand, a more complex one. The thrill of victory had been dampened by the loss he felt in seeing his childhood home destroyed and village annihilated. He had run the gauntlet of emotions, and the day was only half over. A wave of exhaustion engulfed Parker and he leaned back against the trunk for a moment's rest.

As the waning sun began to cast long shadows across the hills, a damaged medical mech approached Parker dozing off under the tree. The Doc extended one of its braided flexible arms and tapped his leg with a delicate metal pincher. Parker shifted his body to avoid being disturbed, but the little robot limped closer and tapped again, this time on his head.

Wearily, Parker grumbled, "Leave me alone."

The Doc pointed to a broken tread on one of his tractor wheels, and Parker waved his hand dismissively. "Shoo, get out of here." But the mech was in a bad way. Its wheel bearings were full of mud, and its circuit relays were crusted over with corrosion. In fact, it had used up most of its emergency power supply trying to locate a tinker for repair. The crippled robot beeped and chirped for assistance. Parker brushed him aside once more. "Buzz off."

The Doc uncoupled the damaged section of track and held it up for Parker to inspect. Irritated, Parker grabbed the tread from the robot and tossed it down the hill. The disappointed mech turned away and slowly began dragging its weather-beaten body over to retrieve the damaged part.

It felt like he had just closed his eyes when he felt another tap on his head. Parker tried to ignore the poking and again shooed the robot away with a flick of his wrist.

"Like I told you before, scat!"

The Doc dropped the damaged tread onto Tilly's utility vest and clicked anxiously for help. The mechanical pleas finally broke through Parker's callous shell and he sat up rubbing his bloodshot eyes.

"All right, all right. You win."

Parker examined the broken link and began to fiddle with it. It was then that he recognized something familiar about the robot and said. "Hey, I remember you. You're that Doc."

The little mech chirped excitedly.

"The one who tried to save the Crinch pilot who was shot down that day," Parker paused. "That crazy day, when I asked Tilly to marry me."

A twinge of compassion pierced through his anesthetized spirit, and he began assessing the Doc's damage.

"Okay, little guy, let's see what you've got." He looked over the mangled mess and commented. "Jiggers, what did you do? Get in an argument with a snuff?"

The Doc huffed an electric buzz.

Parker acknowledged. "Sorry, no offense, but you look about as bad as I feel."

The Doc settled down and waited patiently as Parker pulled a set of tools from Tilly's vest and began working on the twisted tread.

By the time Parker completed repairs on the Doc, the glow of the sun was just beginning to fade. He secured the track into place with a small retaining clip before licking the sleeve of his jacket and buffing a layer of mud off the Doc's spherical head.

Checking over his handiwork, Parker shrugged, "For what it's worth."

The robot tested the traction on the wheel by spinning wildly in a circle.

"Whoa, take it easy or you'll snap that link!"

The Doc took a graceful bow and chirped in appreciation before scurrying down the hillside. Parker stretched his arms and watched the robot disappear into the brush. Leaning back, he noticed Jumbo approaching from over the horizon. Strangely, it felt like old times, and he almost expected to find his sister sitting next to him making small talk and complaining about the old broken hedgehog or some other network snafu.

His hands in his pockets, Jumbo took a seat next to Parker. "I thought I would find you here." He patted an exposed root and smiled. "Old Gurt's still looking good." He reached down and pulled a sprig of dry grass. Slipping it between his teeth, Jumbo reclined against the trunk and reminisced. "Yep, we sure had some good times here."

Parker sat in silence.

"I always thought I'd come back here someday, when the war was over and done with." Jumbo flipped the sprig in his mouth and continued. "You, me, Kiki. Somehow I figured we'd all get back here. Sitting on these lazy hills and watching the days go by," he sighed. "Almost sounds crazy now." Jumbo could see the bleakness in Parker's eyes and asked rhetorically, "You didn't find her, did you?"

Parker shook his head.

"I'm sorry." Jumbo rubbed the back of his neck. "The book says I'm supposed to give you some time off. Bereavement leave, readjustment, or something like that. But the truth is I need you to come back. We need to hold the coast for a long as we can. From what I hear, the Primes are working on something big. I don't have the details yet, but I know we're going to need every available ship in the air when the time comes. If they're right, it could be the bumper blow against the Rud that just might put them out of business for a while."

"What's the point? We're going to lose this war."

Jumbo frowned. "You think so, too, huh?" He slipped the sprig from his mouth. "We're all living on borrowed time."

"Jumbo, what happened? I thought the good guys were supposed to win. Isn't that how it works? Aren't we fighting for a just cause?"

"Good. Bad. History will be recorded by the one with the most firepower."

"But the Crinch are evil. They take whatever they want and give nothing in return. The only thing they create is pain. Don't they realize what they're doing?"

"They're bullies, Parker. And the one thing a bully can't show is weakness. By killing us, they pump up their own ego. They're a sad lot. Tyrannical, arrogant, and rotten to the core."

"Someone needs to punch them in the face."

"Well like I said before, you might just get the chance. But until then, we need to defend ourselves and stay alive."

"Jumbo, all I wanted to do was be a radioman. Nothing special, just do my part and maybe find a little happiness."

"I know," Jumbo agreed. "It's bad luck you got wrapped up in this war. You, of all people, belong somewhere else."

An electronic alarm beeped on Jumbo's chronograph. "It's Squeller. My time's up, and I've gotta get back." Jumbo stood up and dusted off. He plopped his flight helmet back on his head and snapped in the chinstrap. Turning around, he offered Parker a hand. "You coming?"

Parker took a last look at Old Gurdy and the vast devastation surrounding her. Having listened to Jumbo, Parker felt awakened to the truth that they were indeed living on borrowed time, and he now considered himself a member of the dead – no longer fearful of the enemy.

The flight back to Squeller was a somber one. Parker clamped to an empty umbilical near the maintenance pits and saw an eager clerk from intelligence rush over to meet Jumbo as he disembarked in the bay just ahead. There were a few gestures and nods exchanged, and just as swiftly the man was gone.

Over the waning hum of the wakemaker's turbines, Parker heard a whistle from above. He looked up and saw Rex leaning against the handrail raising a large bottle of brill. Exhausted, he waved back as he slowly exited his cockpit. A pair of heavy boots clanked along the footboards from behind, and he felt Jumbo's hand pat him on the shoulder.

"Looks like the welcome wagon's arrived," Jumbo grinned.

Parker nodded and yawned. "Care for a drink?"

"No, thanks. I've got a few things to take care of. You go ahead, but don't get too knackered. Remember, tomorrow's another day."

"I just hope I can make it up to my bunk before I pass out."

"Get some food and some rest," Jumbo advised. "I'll see you in the morning."

He nodded as Jumbo made his way down a corridor. With what little energy he had left, Parker dragged himself up the stairwell and over to his cubby.

Stumbling along the catwalk, Rex greeted Parker with his left arm in a sling. "There's the old harpoon," he grinned, handing Parker the bottle.

Parker quietly gulped a hearty swig.

Rex asked. "Everything all right, bud?"

"Just tired."

"I heard that you swiped a pod this afternoon."

"I had to go check on something."

"Something serious?"

Parker paused before answering, "Nothing I could change."

The alcohol sent a wave of warmth through his body that began to dull his senses. His pain subdued, Parker pointed at Rex's arm and asked, "How about you? That paw's looking a little worse for wear."

"Ah, it's just a little chip off the old block," Rex slurred. "MO says I'll be good as gold in a week."

"All right, ladies." Merv walked over and interrupted. "What is this? A knitting circle?" He popped the lid off the bottle and took a drink. "Come on, let's put some hair on those livers."

"You two go ahead," Parker said. "I think I'm going to pack it in."

"You sure?"

"Maybe next time."

"Well, sleep tight."

"Wake me up when the war is over," Parker said dragging his tired body down the catwalk.

Entering his quarters, Parker took a seat at the edge of the bed. He slipped off his boots and unbuttoned his jacket before collapsing onto the mattress. His mind still swirling with emotion, he wanted nothing more than to forget the events of the day. Triumph and tragedy, it was all too much. Fortunately, exhaustion took over, and within seconds, Parker was fast asleep.

In the days that followed, time passed in a blur, for just as Jumbo had predicted, attacks along the coast were coming in fast and furiously. Parker heeded his friend's advice and did his best to rest his body as much as possible but above all else, bring his wakemaker back at any and all costs. However, despite his and the squadron's best effort, by the end of the month, Button Blue was down to its last four ships and had seen an equal number of pilots killed during this time. The first week was the hardest, and Parker wasn't sure if he would be able to survive the unending gauntlet of constant combat. Though strangely, by the end of the second, he didn't feel much of anything anymore. He was simply going through the motions, day after day, until it felt as if he was flying more on instinct than skill. He did, nevertheless, manage to string up an additional three confirmed kills during this time – two bombers and a fighter. In addition to his aerial achievements, Parker had also made it through a barrel's worth of brew and a case of brown brill and felt as if he had aged ten years. But that was of no matter because in his mind there was nothing left to live for.

Upon completion of their hundredth sortie, the squadron went out to celebrate in the town of Whisker. It was the first full day off they had had in weeks, and they were all itching to get out of the "dungeon," and back into civilization.

They headed over to the local drey to share stories of their perils with death, and joked blithely about the pathetic condition of the remaining fighters left in their possession. Both Parker and Rex were now recorded veterans, but poor Merv, who was so focused on becoming a hero, still hadn't earned even a partial kill to his credit. As they spent the day eating and drinking to their hearts' content, an ominous feeling began to weigh heavily on the squadron. The rumor of Air Armory's planned offensive was now less a matter of "if" but rather a matter of "when," and it was almost a guarantee that the pilots of Button Blue would be the first to venture over.

Stocked to the gills and bellies full, the group staggered out of the brewery. As they made their way to an awaiting transport, Rex caught sight of an enemy pulsejet. He lifted his arms as if holding a rifle and mimicked taking shots at the aircraft as it streamed overhead.

"Rat, tat, tat, tat, tat," Rex burst in staccato.

He twisted his body in a circle and tried to keep a lead on the target but soon lost his balance and stumbled headfirst into a pole. Collapsing onto the cobblestone road, he grimaced in pain as the other pilots lifted him from the ground. Hunching over, Rex grabbed his left arm and shouted, "Jiggers! That hurts!"

Parker could see that Rex's previously injured shoulder had been dislocated and quickly shuffled Rex into the transport.

Within the hour, the group was back at Squeller, and Rex staggered his way to the infirmary, while Parker and the rest of the pilots made their way back into the complex. When the group arrived back at the flight deck, Parker immediately realized something was different. Looking out amongst the concourse, he saw that there was not a single aircraft docked along the railing. He turned to Merv and asked, "Hey, what happened to all the kites?"

Merv rubbed his eyes and shrugged. "Who cares? Maybe the Crinch surrendered."

"Cheers to that," Parker nodded.

"Nighty night, mother goose," Merv yawned.

"Happy landings."

Parker pushed the button under his name placard and the door to his quarters slid open. The old concrete sled with its quilted mattress beckoned him to rest his weary body. Without even removing his boots, Parker flopped face first onto his bunk and was unconscious before his head hit the pillow.

Early next morning, Paddock awoke Parker with a gentle tap on the back.

"Morning, sir. Sleep well?"

"Still asleep," Parker groaned.

As he sat up, he felt an intense pain clamping around his skull.

"Congrats again on netting the big fiver the other day," Paddock complimented. "I took the liberty of posting the marks on your new wake."

"New wake?" Parker questioned, his eyes half-closed.

"The whole squadron's been recycled for strike detail and reconfigured to Class-B," Paddock said. "I switched out your old radio receiver with a new booster, and in case you're keeping score, I counted twenty-three holes in your last outing."

Parker slipped into his boots and rose slowly from his bunk.

"Briefing is at o-eight-hundred. If you need me, I'll be bivouacking on C deck."

"Briefing? What briefing?" Parker asked.

"For the kickoff, sir," Paddock said. "Bad weather's coming in, so word just came down from the AP that the strike's been moved up."

"Wonderful," Parker said sarcastically, rubbing the temples of his head. "Do you think I have time for a shower?"

Paddock tossed him a towel and placed a canister of hot tea on the desk.

"You're a lifesaver," Parker said thankfully.

"Good luck, sir," Paddock saluted. "Blow 'em buzzards a kiss for me."

The conference room was buzzing with excitement as the capacity forum eagerly awaited details of the day's mission. Jumbo entered and made his way to the front.

"Good morning."

He flipped the switch on a large display panel that illuminated a tactical map of the Downy coastline.

"I know most of you already have a pretty good idea of where we're going today, so I'll keep this short." He pulled out a thin pointing rod and tapped one of the markers on the display. The picture zoomed in on a highlighted target area.

"Intel has spotted a Crinch metal works factory located in the southwest sector of Collier near the Antweer Strait. The factory is located within the confines of a forced labor camp. It is our job today to strike the target at this precise point."

A red border outlined a long rectangular warehouse, and a small dot blinked over a pair of smokestacks.

"As you already know, many of our own are being held captive within these walls, and some of them may be injured by our actions. But it is imperative to the survival of our country and our people that this task is done. Bear that in mind as you make your run. Try your best to split the crosshairs on this one and keep the collateral damage down to a minimum. Now, the bulk of the manufacturing is done underground, so this will be a combined strike led by bombers from Mallard Group."

Jumbo looked over to a gritty, stubble-faced man sitting slouched in the back corner of the room with his arms folded.

"Popper, you and your crews will be responsible for the above-ground clearing. Once you've softened them up, the remaining escorts will fly in and hit the exposed factory with rotters stolen from the Crinch." With a sly wink, he added, "Now, that oughta sour their puckers." A cheerful rouse broke out. "But don't forget, it's extremely corrosive stuff, and if any of your ships are hit during the run, be sure to dive out of formation and salvo immediately."

Jumbo touched off the screen.

"Button Blue pilots, note that you'll be wrangling Class-B's today, so beware of the extra weight, and slower response."

Jumbo looked out amongst the sea of faces staring back at him and knew that many would not be there the following day. "More skeletons for the closet," he thought to himself.

Clearing his throat, Jumbo concluded the briefing. "For a lot of us, this will be a new experience. It's the first offensive strike we've taken against the Crinch since we scuttled out of Downy with our tails between our legs. Set your chronometers on my mark." He clicked a dial on the face of his watch. "Mark. Takeoff is at zero nine hundred. Stay sharp up there, and good luck."

A group's adjutant rose from his chair and said, "Attention!"

The bustling gallery stood up as Jumbo exited the briefing. "Dismissed."

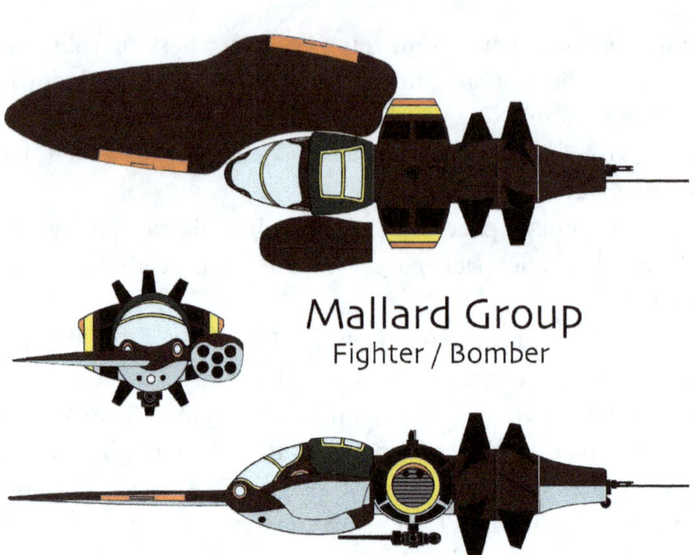

Mallard Group
Fighter / Bomber

Along the catwalk, Parker caught sight of his newly configured wakemaker. The bulky bomber was a very different beast compared to the stout dragonfly-shaped interceptor he was used to flying.

The main stabilizer was contoured in the shape of a piercing shark fin and fitted with two sets of magnetic hardpoints loaded with bombs. On the other side of the cockpit, an added gun pod brimmed with a half-dozen tubes that housed targeting sensors, flare launchers, and of course, cannons. A tumbler canon was mounted at the rear of the end cap, while a ground-attack strafing slinger was housed underneath. All together, they combined to form quite a menacing looking fortress.

From the doorway of his cubby, Rex shuffled over to greet Parker.

"Head still spinning?" Parker asked.

Rubbing his eyes, Rex said, "No, the head's fine. It's the floor that won't stand still." He popped a couple of tablets and swallowed them dry.

"Well, we did get pretty bent yesterday."

"Like a pretzel."

"I heard the M.O. grounded you?"

Rex leaned tenderly with his shoulder. "Yeah, tough to punch the throttle."

"Lucky duck," Parker smiled, continuing with his preflight check. "So, here to send me off?"

"I'll do you one better. I'm going with you."

"Wait? I thought you were grounded?"

"Well, I might not be able to fly. But I still got my trigger finger."

"Meaning what? You're trading your wings in for a pee-shooter?"

"Sure, why not?"

Parker laughed. "You dizzy lush. In the shape you're in? The last thing the group needs right now is you taking pot shots at them."

"Are you kidding? You know, I always track best when I'm a little tilted. I just close my eyes and squeeze. Besides, it's a well-known fact that my left eye's a bit nutty, so the brill will help me from getting twitchy."

"I don't know, Rex. Sounds like it's going to be a little rough. You got the day off. You should take it."

"There'll be plenty of down time later. They say if this plan works, we could put a dent in the Crinch war machine. I can't miss this party."

Parker took a moment to assess the situation.

Rex continued, "Come on, who do you want upstairs with you when the chips are down? Some greenhorn ninny soaking in wet naps and crying out for his mama? Or me?"

"Doesn't your mother love you?" Parker joked.

"That's another story," Rex chuckled. "Come on, let's pack it in."

Against his better judgment, Parker agreed. He figured Rex would probably tag along anyway, and it was better to have him close rather than make him link up with another unit. Together, the two snapped into their chutes and climbed aboard.

Interior-wise, the bomber's layout felt relatively familiar, though the size of the two-man cockpit was much larger and roomier. Both the pilot and gunner sat upright instead of cradled, and there was plenty of space between the chairs and fuselage. All the flight controls and forward weapons systems were attached along the side armrests, and a series of targeting scopes were mounted above at the periphery of the pilot's vision. Adjusting the display angle on the short-range radar, Parker pulled down on the padded horse collar and ratcheted it into place. He flicked a few switches and adjusted the pressure settings before engaging the starter. A thunderous roar shook the pod as the turbines stirred to life.

As the engines revved to speed, the vibration slowly subsided and both men completed their checklist. Parker adjusted the microphone to his lips and ran a quick voice check through the intercom.

"She's warming up, Rex. Are you set?"

Rex stifled a sickly belch and pounded his chest with his fist. "Bottoms up."

Parker reached down to the umbilical release. "Safety catch off."

"Clear in the rear," Rex confirmed.

Parker pulled the handle and the hydraulic docking clamp disengaged from the main stabilizer. "Umbilical detached, all moorings clear."

Rex mimicked a hunting call over the intercom and shouted, "Tallyho!"

As Parker nudged the throttle forward, the heavily weighted bomber slowly accelerated from the hangar.

Soaring above the channel, Parker brought his wakemaker alongside Jumbo and Merv. Three new rookies – Notch,

Tubs, and Daft – completed the escort squadron. A few clicks ahead, a strike force of heavy bombers led by Squadron Leader Popper lumbered toward the province of Downy. There were twelve in all, grouped tightly together in a box formation that glided over the white-capped sea twinkling like a blanket of stars.

As they neared the target, a navigator broadcast an update over the radio. "Vector one one five and continue descent to flight level two thousand. Reduce speed to three five zero. Standby for I.P.–"

Merv's voice crackled in and interrupted the report. "Enemy contact, two o'clock low!"

Jumbo scanned the area and spotted the enemy flight. "I see them," he confirmed. "Parker, you and Tubs take the left. Merv and I will hit the right. The rest of you fly down and protect the bombers. Scatter!"

The squadron broke up into three separate flights and dove into their assigned positions.

As Parker zeroed in on an enemy intercept, a signal lit up on Rex's display.

"Parker! Back door contact, six o'clock high!"

Parker notified his wingman, "Tubs, check your tail. We've got company!"

"My scope's negative. Are you sure?"

Tracer fire streamed past the windshield.

"I'm sure! He's right on top of us! Scramble!" Parker shouted.

The pair broke formation. Tubs pulled his bomber high but a direct hit in his pressurized fuel cell blew him apart into a thousand bits. The blast rocked Parker from behind and sent his ship spiraling downward. As he struggled to regain control, a trail of bullets riddled through the cockpit.

"Rex, I can't beat him! You've gotta get a fix!"

Looking through a periscope, Rex frantically searched the skies for a target. "I'm working on it!"

An alert flashed, and Parker felt a sudden drop in airspeed. He checked the gauges and saw they were losing pressure.

"I think we've sprung a leak!"

"Break right!" Rex yelled.

Parker yanked the control stick hard and sent the bomber into a roll. As they tumbled over, Rex managed to get a momentary lock on the pursuing fighter. He fired a volley of darts into the enemy's pulsejet engine and pumped his fist as the fighter burst into flames.

"Gotcha!" he exclaimed.

"Nice shot!" Parker cheered as he leveled the wakemaker upright and angled around to regroup.

In another part of the sky, Jumbo was tangled in a dogfight of his own. He edged in for a clean shot behind a Crinch interceptor. Pulling the trigger on his control stick, he could feel the recoil from the cannons rattling bolts of death across the buzzard's silhouette. Bits of metal splintered off the enemy as Jumbo lined up for the kill. The target filling his sights, he squeezed again. A few rounds popped before the guns inexplicably jammed. Jumbo tapped the trigger and pleaded, "Come on, come on!" He tried resetting the pressure in the main lines and toggled through the weapons selector, but still nothing happened. Over the intercom, Jumbo called out, "Merv, where are you?"

"I'm right behind you, boss."

"I've got a gremlin in my guns! Switch up and give 'em a quick burst."

"Copy, Leader."

Jumbo reduced his throttle as Merv pushed ahead to take the lead. Targeting the fighter, he engaged his gun pod and scored a light hit. A trail of black smoke sputtered from the enemy's exhaust port. Edging in closer, Merv fired again. A red splatter smeared across the inside of the enemy's cockpit.

"Jiggers!" Merv cringed as the Crinch fighter spiraled downward.

"Stay focused, Button Four," Jumbo ordered. "Descend down to the deck and line up on the I.P."

Merv took a deep breath and steadied his nerves. "Copy, Leader."

Puffs of anti-aircraft flak dotted the sky ahead as several bombers from the first group were shot down in quick succession. Jumbo leveled out just above the tree line and radioed, "Mallard Leader, you're clear to target."

"Get ready for a show," Popper acknowledged. Settling in on the bomb run, he relayed a final bit of encouragement to the group. "All right, you quacks, get ready to lay those eggs. Salvo in three, two, one. Drop!" He pulled the bomb release and felt his ship rise upward as the heavy ordinance fell onto the target and blew a gaping crater in the center of the complex.

Over the intercom, Jumbo congratulated Popper, "Nice kick in the door, Pop! The first round's on me. Exit at vector two seven zero. You should have a clear line home."

"Copy, Button Leader. See you back in the barn."

Jumbo turned to his wingman. "All right, Merv. Let's get in there." He scanned the sky for the rest of the squadron and called out for Parker. "Button Three, where are you?"

Parker swooped in from above. "Coming in off your starboard bow."

Jumbo looked to his right and saw Parker diving in alongside, alone. "I see you, but where's Tubs?" he asked.

Parker signaled to Jumbo a thumbs-down.

"Understood. Throttle down and slide in the back door."

Parker acknowledged and slotted into the rear of the formation. Lining up on the bomb run, he removed the safety catch from his bomb release and set the rotters to salvo. With his eye pressed against the bombsight, he was shocked to see the devastation that lay ahead. It was a horrible scene filled with countless bodies of the dead and dying, factory workers and prisoners alike, all scattered about – burned, mutilated, and bloodied by shrapnel.

His stomach churned with disgust as he made a final fix on the drop zone. His palms were slick and his fingers twitched while he rested his hand along the bomb release handle and waited for the command to drop.

Jumbo's voice bellowed over the intercom, "All right, keep sharp, this is it!"

Parker held his breath as the smoldering factory edged closer. Through the rushing landscape, he spotted a lone figure standing in the middle of the target area. Parker adjusted focus on the bombsight and saw what appeared to be a prisoner dressed in tattered flight gear looking in his direction.

Parker shouted, "Jumbo, delay the strike! The factory's not clear!"

"Negative! You know the mission! Now get ready to drop!"

"But they're using our own as fodder!"

"You knew that before we left. Now form up!"

Despite his feelings of guilt, Parker knew this was the only way to stop the spreading plague of Crinch domination. He settled into formation and confirmed. "I'm in."

The squadron was now set and just moments away from releasing their bombs. A barrage of anti-aircraft fire blasted from below and hit one of the rotting canisters secured to Merv's wakemaker.

"I'm hit!" Merv shouted.

The leaking gas began melting away the ship's thin metal plating.

"Salvo and get clear!" Jumbo ordered.

Merv pulled the release handle but found bombs fused into place.

"I can't! The circuit's melted!"

A series of warning lights flashed on his panel as the propellers on his spinner screeched to a halt.

"I just lost my secondary!"

"Bail out!"

Sounds of twisting metal screeched through the cockpit as Merv struggled to eject. There was a terrible snap, and the wakemaker's main stabilizer ripped away from the side of the fuselage. "She's coming apart!"

Under the intense air pressure, the ship folded in half and crumbled to the ground in a smoldering heap.

Parker turned away from the gruesome sight as a message broadcast over his headset. "Button three, close up."

Parker pushed his throttle forward and slotted into Merv's position. With stern concentration, he grabbed the bomb release and waited for the command.

"Drop!" Jumbo ordered.

Parker pulled on the handle and felt the canisters fall away. A moment later, a blast rumbled in the background.

Jumbo cursed with an angry update. "Damn it! We overshot the target!"

Just beyond the factory, a cloud of white gas washed over a mass of prisoners. The toxic smoke sent dozens of people collapsing to the ground with only a fortunate few being able to escape upwind where there were still pockets of fresh air.

Disgusted, Jumbo slammed his fist against the instrument panel. Gritting his teeth, he turned his attention to a second attack on the factory's power plant. "Parker, pressure up and follow me. We may have missed the main target but we can still take out that generator."

"Copy, Leader,'" Parker replied, angling in on the strike.

The two wakemakers glided gracefully upward before diving in for a ground attack.

Parker called over his shoulder, "Rex, get ready to light it up!"

"I see it." Rex edged the crosshairs over the target. "Coming into range."

Through the smoke of the battlefield, Parker again noticed the figure standing in the center of the compound. He did not know if what he saw was real or a mirage, but a great gravity pulled him from within.

The outside world fell silent as Parker whispered his sister's name, "Kiki?"

Bursting with elation, he blurted, "She's alive!"

The unexpected discovery reignited Parker's dream of fulfilling his promise and returning his sister home. The joy he felt, however, was abruptly halted when the thundering blast of the strafing cannon jolted him back to his senses. Sparks flew as high-caliber darts pounded the power generator ahead and engulfed the low-flying bomber in an expanding ball of fire.

"Pull up!" Rex shouted, as a searing cloud of shrapnel smashed through the cockpit's forward windshield and blinded Parker in a shower of broken glass. Wailing alarms and a heavy jolt signaled that the bomber's main turbine had been severely damaged.

"We're losing pressure!"

"I can't see!" Parker shouted. "Are we clear?"

Parker struggled to keep the bomber airborne as smoke filled the cabin.

"She's going to fold!" Rex panicked.

"I can't find my kicker!" Parker yelled. "Rex, you're going to have to punch us out!"

Rex reached down and pulled up on a brightly painted ejection lever. He held his breath and clenched his eyes shut as the top and forward windshields were blown clear with explosive bolts.

Parker tucked his chin and held his breath as the pneumatically charged seat shot out of the forward canopy and into the rushing air.

Jumbo caught sight of the two chutes deploying just beyond the factory. He turned to his gunner and said, "Horley, pressure up! We're going to do a pick up."

"Ready, Skip!" the gunner replied.

Touching down just beyond the perimeter of the camp, Parker could hear his wakemaker crash into the nearby forest.

Rex detached from his chute and rushed over to assist Parker, who could not see.

"Parker, we have to get out of here!"

Blood squeezed from the corners of Parker's eyes. "Where are we?"

"Where we definitely shouldn't be."

Parker tried to flee but felt one of his boots sinking deep in the mud. "My leg. It's stuck."

"Give me your hand!"

Rex pulled hard until Parker's foot finally popped free. His ankle sprained and throbbing, Parker threw his arm around Rex's shoulder and the two hobbled away as fast as they could.

As they neared the forest, rustling foliage could be heard breaking through the tree line.

"What's that sound?" Parker asked.

Rex looked up and saw an armored plated sentinel breaking through the brush ahead and gulped. "I think we're in trouble."

Inside the camp, prisoners and guards alike scrambled to find cover from the corrosive inferno of rotting gas. They dashed about, huddling for cover under broken pieces of timber and behind heavy machinery. Some of the more daring used the opportunity to escape. Delirious, a lemming-like mass of prisoners stormed the main gate, only to have their legs shattered by the grenade-like hobblers clamped around their ankles. From the middle of the compound, Kiki could see each victim fall to the sinister snare. She covered her ears with her hands but could not tune out the terrible cries of the maimed.

She rushed over and tried to help the wounded, making sure all the while she maintained a safe distance from the perimeter. As she laced a makeshift tourniquet around the leg of an injured prisoner, she spotted two white parachutes fluttering along the ground and not far away, two pilots rushing into the forest. Remembering the desperation felt in those last moments of freedom before being captured, she projected all her hopes to their safety and rescue.

Watching the two men hop three-legged into the brush, Kiki noticed something oddly familiar in the shape and movement of one of the pilots. Instantly, she recognized who it was and shouted at the top of her lungs, "Parker!"

Kiki's voice pierced through the raucous pandemonium and stopped Parker dead in his tracks.

With the sentinels closing in, Rex warned, "Move it, Parker! They're right behind us!"

Parker pulled away from Rex's grip and dashed blindly back in the direction of the camp.

"Parker, what are you doing?"

"Kiki!" he screamed.

Rex rushed back and tackled his friend to the ground.

"You're going the wrong way!"

Consumed by the obsession to save his sister, Parker continued crawling his way in the direction of his sister's voice.

Rex grabbed Parker by the shoulder and shook him violently. "Listen to me! Parker, we're in deep! We gotta get out of here!"

"No!" Parker shouted defiantly.

Rex scanned the trees and saw the sentinels moving in from multiple directions.

"They've got us flanked!"

"Get out of here, Rex!"

"Just shut up and move!"

"It's no good. I can't run."

"Then hop!"

The sentinels surrounded the pilots and closed in for the kill. Rex spun around like a cornered animal looking for an escape, but found none. Realizing there was no way out, Rex kneeled down to the ground and raised his uninjured arm over his head in a gesture of surrender.

"What's happening?" Parker asked.

Rex said nothing. He was too busy contemplating the fate that awaited them. He wondered whether they would be sent into forced labor or just simply killed. Mustering as much courage as he could, Rex faced his fate with his eyes wide open.

The lead sentinel slowly lowered the sharpened tip of one of its appendages onto Rex's chest and prepared to thrust it through. As Rex sneered at his captor, a twinkle of light reflected off the sentinel's armor plating as a flurry of darts riddled the robot like a rag doll. Rex fell to the ground and covered his head as the hailstorm of cannon fire wiped out the entire patrol.

The roar of a turbine rumbled overhead. Rex looked up and saw Jumbo's wakemaker hovering in for a landing.

He cheered with joy and clasped his hands in gratitude. "Thank you!"

Settling onto the murky soil, the slender landing gear began slowly sinking into the mud as Jumbo exited the cockpit. He hopped down from the main stabilizer and dashed over to help his fallen friends.

"I could kiss you, sir!" Rex greeted him.

"Thanks, but you're not my type," Jumbo smiled. "I hope you two didn't have a big breakfast. It's going to be a tight squeeze."

He hoisted Rex up onto the sturdy metal fin, and together they managed to lift Parker onto the wing.

"Jumbo, she's alive!"

"What are you talking about?" Jumbo asked. "Who?"

But before Parker could respond, another squad of sentinels broke through the woods. The sound of bullets ricocheted off the fuselage while Horley pulled Parker into the cockpit.

Rex fell flat onto the main stabilizer to avoid being shot. He crawled to the edge and reached down to lend Jumbo a hand. Another stream of bullets splattered across the bomber, and he heard an agonizing groan bellow from below. A warm ooze slicked over Rex's fingers as Jumbo's hand slipped from his grip.

Peering over the edge, he saw Jumbo hunched over in a puddle of blood.

"Sir, you've gotta help me!" Rex shouted. "You've gotta try and stand up!"

Jumbo did his best to push himself up from the ground.

Rex grabbed him by the collar and pulled with all his might. But the weight was too much for him to lift alone. Losing hold of his grip, Rex watched as Jumbo's body collapsed back onto the ground.

Clutching his stomach, Jumbo commanded, "Get out of here! Don't let them capture you. That's an order!"

More bullets riddled across the pod.

Out of options and out of reach, Rex scurried into the cockpit. He yanked down the safety harness and revved the engines for takeoff. With an agonizing push of the throttle, he called out to Horley, "Kid, pressure up and give me cover!"

"Where's the skipper?" Horley asked.

There was no response. Only the strained whistling of the blower's turbine could be heard as it desperately tried to free itself from the sticky mud.

"Rex! Where's Jumbo?" Parker asked.

The bomber slowly lifted into the air, and Parker pushed his face up against the side window to look out. His vision blurred and crimson, he could just make out the outline of a body surrounded by a circle of sentinels. His heart sank as he watched his old friend writhing in pain. "Jumbo!" Parker shouted. He grabbed the back of the pilot's chair and demanded, "Rex, we've got to go back!"

"It's too late, Parker!"

"We can't leave him! It's not right! He came back for us!"

Parker reached for the throttle but was blasted back by an explosive round that pierced through the pod's fuselage.

Rex struggled to keep the wakemaker airborne. "Parker, we're all going to be goners if we don't get the hell out of here!"

"But it's not right!"

"I'm sorry, bud. But we're history."

Rex snapped the secondary props into gear and jolted the wakemaker away from the battlefield.

The beleaguered bomber fading from view, Jumbo edged a wry smile to his friends as they made their way back to safety.

A crowd gathered around the main gate as the sentinels returned with their bounty. Lumbering across the grounds, the lead robot dropped the wounded pilot in the center of the courtyard. Kiki pushed her way to the front and saw Jumbo's body covered in blood. She dashed to his side and kneeled next to him. She wiped the mud from his face and whispered, "Jumbo, can you hear me?"

He peeked his eyes open and gazed at her in disbelief. "I must be dead or dreaming. Is it really you?"

"You're not dead. Or dreaming. It's me. I'm here."

She kissed him gently on the forehead.

"I'm sorry, Keek. I should have believed him," Jumbo wept.

Kiki placed her fingers across his lips and hushed. "Don't worry about that now. Just lay still and be quiet."

The dark shadow of the camp commander loomed overhead. He was an aged and stony man who stood tall and menacingly rigid. Bundled in a thick wool overcoat and wearing a pair of black leather boots, his gaunt pale face lay shrouded under the sharp bill of an officer's cap. He moved closer to investigate and slowly nudged Jumbo with his foot.

Kiki lowered her head in submission as Jumbo played possum.

Aware of the anxious anticipation brewing in the audience, the commander lifted his foot and placed pressure upon Jumbo's midsection. An eerie squish exuded as he twisted the sole of his boot onto Jumbo's exposed innards.

The pressure too excruciating, Jumbo squirmed in agony in search of relief from the intolerable pain.

Kiki grabbed the officer's leg and struggled to keep him at bay. She clawed and pulled but soon fell victim to a sudden blow from the blunt stock of a rifle and crumpled to the ground. She felt her energy wane as an intravenous relay was torn from her arteries. The tubes squirted blood and other fluids wildly through the air. She desperately rushed to reconnect the hoses that maintained her sustenance.

The Commander scanned the faces of the prisoners as they watched the scene unfold with lurid curiosity.

The warden pushed ever harder on Jumbo's belly, until he finally let out a terrible roar before falling unconscious.

Releasing pressure, the Commander wiped the sole of his boot against the side of Jumbo's face. With a single wave of his hand, the guards retrieved a coil of rope. Together with the sentinels' assistance, they bound Jumbo like a captured animal and hoisted his body up a pole as a warning for all to see. A trickle of rain began to sprinkle down from an overcast sky. Satisfied with the effectiveness of his demonstration, the warden turned around and headed back to the bunkhouse located at the far end of the compound.

Eventually, the prisoners dispersed, and Kiki was dragged away and tossed into a nearby cooler located in the middle of the compound.

Through the bars of the exposed ceiling, she pulled her head above ground level and saw Jumbo's tattered body swaying in the wind. Drops of rain mixed with her tears and edged into the corners of her mouth. Losing grip, she dropped to the floor.

Curled up in a corner of the cell, she did her best to focus on memories of happier times. She recalled the scent of Old Gurdy and could almost feel the sprigs of tall grass brushing against her body. Her mind drifted from the present to the past and back again as she asked her mother, her father, and all the spirits before that simple yet unanswerable question: "Why?"

Spring

Trapped in a world of darkness, Parker did his best to remain calm as a pair of robotic arms worked to repair his vision. An ocular probe gently tugged on his eyelids and injected an anesthetic. A sudden stream of light shot into his retina and blinded him with brightness. He felt a quick succession of needle-sharp pricks as tiny pinchers pried layers of torn tissue apart and extracted shards of glass from his cornea. After all the bits had been removed, the robotic surgeon sprayed a jet of antibiotic gel over the surface of his eyes and completed the procedure by layering a mask of gauze over his lids.

Many hours passed before Parker became conscious again. He was not sure exactly how long he had been asleep or what time of day it was, but from the sound of foot traffic passing outside his cubby, he assumed it must be daylight. Though his eyes were still sore and tender to the touch, he removed the patches against the doctor's orders. At first, he saw only a soft gray blur, but that was enough to provide him with a sense of relief, for at least to some degree, his sight had been restored.

He placed a hand in front of his face and squinted to focus. He could see the fuzzy outline of his fingers forming a silhouette against the glow of light reflecting through the door. He heard a pair of riggers enjoying some light conversation along the catwalk and wondered just how much time he had squandered in recovery. After a few minutes, things started to sharpen back to normal, and Parker decided it was time to get out of bed.

He rose to his feet with the help of a chair. He took a few steps to check the strength of his legs. Every muscle in his body ached and he could feel a twinge of pain in his right ankle. Gently, he slipped into his boots and buttoned up his tunic before collecting his flight anorak and pulling it over his head. Upon balancing himself away from the chair, he slowly hobbled out of the warm confines of his quarters and onto the promenade.

Nauseous from the anesthesia, Parker decided that it might do him good to get some fresh air before eating. He walked to a nearby lift and took it all the way up to the surface. Cold sea air rushed in as the elevator doors opened.

Spotting a tall sonic array erected at the end of the observation platform, Parker ventured over and climbed to the top. Perched high in the crow's nest, he looked out amongst the rocky jetty. Rays of sunbeams broke through the passing clouds and danced in a kaleidoscope of light across a valley of green in the distance. The tall fertile grass waved in rhythmic patterns across the ground in gentle harmony with the offshore breeze.

"So much beauty," Parker thought. "The world still blooms, even during these darkest of days."

He followed a trail of light that glided across the plains in a dreamlike spectacle, and noticed a familiar image of the Griffin and the Ghost. Parker was spellbound as the duo drifted along the earthen incline and softly disappeared from view.

When the moment was over, Parker was struck by an odd sensation, a feeling of déjà vu. He knew this moment was somehow connected to his past, or maybe it was his future, all the while pressing, trying to invoke some indomitable image imprinted deep within his memory. He rubbed his swollen eyes and waited patiently, hoping for some sign that would enlighten him to the purpose of the vision.

As he pondered the dismal state of his existence, he wondered what other wretchedness was lurking in the shadows. Most of those closest to him were already dead, and though he took refuge in the knowledge that his sister was still alive, her freedom was still very much in doubt. The attempt to rescue Kiki would be a perilous one, one that even the most intrepid of gamblers would not venture to wager.

He remembered the days spent training in the glen and the conversations he had with his father regarding the quality of one's character and the importance of intention. It was now vividly clear what his father meant when he explained all those years earlier the value of losing. Parker had had his fill of death. Tilly, Smilie, his parents, Jumbo, Merv, Notch, Skink, and a myriad of others were all gone. Only Kiki remained. She was the only thing left worth living for, and Parker made a solemn pledge that saving her would be his final deed. He would go back to Downy and prevail, or at the very least the game would be over. Gazing upon the Rutlan Jetty, Parker finally understood his place in the world, his role in the fight, and the senseless brutality that was the nature of war.

Alone in his cubby, Parker finished final preparations for his clandestine mission. He snapped into his flight gear and from under his bunk pulled out Tilly's tattered utility vest and an old set of hoppers. As he stuffed them into a kitbag, a small photo fluttered onto the ground. Parker picked it up and wiped off a layer of dust from across his pant leg. Holding it up to the light, he noticed it was a snapshot of Kiki working on an old sonic array back at Kakydurn and giving him the familiar stink eye. Parker felt it ironic that this tiny image had captured the pivotal moment when the course of his life changed – the day when Kiki decided to leave home.

"Funny how a single choice could alter the lives of so many," Parker thought.

There was a knock at the entry; Parker saw Rex peering into his quarters. He shuffled the picture into his lapel pocket and pulled the ties closed on the sack.

"Tell me all your ducks are lined up and that you don't just have a screw loose?" Rex remarked.

"What do you mean?"

"The CO grounded you for a week. So I'm wondering: Why is it that your name is back up on the board? Are you crazy?"

"Crazy like a fox," Parker grinned. "I talked with the MO and he gave me the go-ahead. So I guess I'm fit to fly."

Rex looked at the sorry figure standing before him and shook his head. "Buddy, you're not fit to breathe."

"Well, it's a good thing you're not a doctor, because he gave me the green light."

"That daft old bugger gives everyone the go-ahead. Heck, he'd toss his own mother into the air if he could pin wings on her back and give her a swift kick in the rump. But you, I could weld a spinner to your head, and you'd still be grounded."

"I won't argue with that. I could probably sleep a month and not even shake for a tinkle… Still, I'm going back."

"It's a one-way ticket." Rex cautioned. "We lost half the group on the last run. You coming along would just be adding more fuel to the fire."

"It's not a choice. I have to go."

"There'll be plenty of other missions. Why choose this one?"

Parker twirled Kiki's old spigot between his fingers and said, "Because I've lost enough."

Parker's voice was firm, and though Rex wanted to stop his friend from making a rash decision, he knew there was nothing he could say or do that would change Parker's mind.

"Suit yourself." Rex huffed and turned to leave. "But just for the record, I think you're a damn fool."

"Rex…"

"…Yeah?"

"Thank you."

"For what?"

"For being my friend." Parker recalled their previous outing. "I'm sorry for barking at you the other day. I know it wasn't your fault. It's just that… It seems like everywhere I go, people keep dying all around me."

"I know," Rex said. "Jumbo was your friend, and he deserved better. Hell, they all deserved better. I guess this rotation ain't quite the cakewalk I thought it'd be. It's more like pound cake with a slice of humble pie." Rex shrugged, "Life, huh? What a pisser." Then with a forced smile, he added. "I'll see you upstairs."

Parker watched as Rex exited. It felt good to clear the air, especially before the mission. He gathered the rest of his supplies and slung the bag over his shoulder. Folding the sheet back neatly on his bunk, Parker patted the picture in his pocket for good luck before heading out to the flight deck.

It was the final sortie in the big push and Air Armory was sending up everything left in its arsenal that could fly. The hope was that a single overwhelming offensive across a wide section of targets would result in a temporary halt to the juggernaut that was the Crinch war machine. Like a handful of pebbles thrown into a pond, it was anticipated that this attack would reverberate across the entire nation of Downy and give the underground resistance a chance to liberate itself from the tyranny of its ruthless oppressor.

Again, the metal works factory was chosen as the primary target for the group at Squeller. Both Parker and Rex had volunteered to run point on the initial engagement and clear a path for the others to follow.

Making his way down the catwalk, Parker saw Jumbo's wakemaker docked along an umbilical and felt a deep sense of remorse. His thoughts shifted, however, when Paddock rushed over to greet him. "Congratulations, Flight Lieutenant," Paddock said. "Nice to see you back in the shed."

"Lieutenant?" The new title caught Parker by surprise. He looked down at the rank insignia patched across his chest. Indeed, he had been promoted. Parker had no recollection of the event or exactly when it happened, but in all fairness, he did not remember much of anything that had occurred over the last few days.

"So, how does she look?" Parker asked.

"About as good as forty-eight plugs, three windshields, and a pair of new cranks can."

Parker examined the newly installed sona-pod attached below the ship's blower before hopping up onto the main stabilizer.

"Think she'll hold together?"

"Well, she's a buxom broad, but she ain't much to look at anymore. Truth be told, this little lady's been pounded well past her prime."

Settling into the pilot's chair, Parker reached for the satchel of gear.

"Planning a picnic, sir?"

"Just a little insurance."

Parker flipped on the charging coils, and the wakemaker's electric generators began to whir. Paddock covered his ears and shouted a few last-minute details. "Just to let you know, those thirties pack a big punch, but you only have about ten seconds of firing time. Also, I switched out the old blades with a couple of new spinners. They oughta give you a nice kick!"

Parker signaled thumbs up.

"Good luck, sir. Sock it to 'em!"

As the forward windshield folded downward, Parker engaged the turbines, and the ship roared to life. Paddock waved with great enthusiasm as the heavy metal clamp detached from the main stabilizer. With a gentle push of the throttle, the additional blades on the new pusher-props revved up to speed and accelerated the fatigued bomber out of the hangar.

The skies over the water were dark and ominous. Parker set the auto-nav and scanned the area for enemy fighters. He expected a clear run to the target since the weather ahead was projected to be equally poor. Bustling wind shears shook his wakemaker and bounced him about the cockpit like a rag doll.

It took less than an hour to reach the Downy Coast, more than enough time to rustle up butterflies in Parker's stomach. As he and Rex approached the shoreline, a series of blips flashed on the forward display.

"Rex, are you there?" Parker radioed.

"Right behind you."

"I'm picking up an active array, twelve points out. Let's head over and get a jump on it."

"Copy, Leader."

With a flick of his thumb, Parker flipped up the trigger guard and prepared for an attack.

They leveled out just above the ground and closed into a tight formation. A curtain of heavy rain crackled against the forward windshield and made visibility extremely poor. Through the waves of rippling water, Parker noticed a tiny flash twinkling in the distance. At first, he thought it might be a beacon or reflection, but the thudding bullets and streams of tracer fire indicated otherwise.

"Zipper!" Parker shouted.

Immediately, the two pilots dodged their ships evasively as they approached the first target. Parker struggled to keep the enemy battery centered in his sights when one of the hydraulic lines in his main stabilizer was severed. Tightening his grip on the control stick with both hands, he managed to get a momentary lock on the battery and pulled the trigger. The gun-pod made quick work of the anti-aircraft array and sent it crumbling down in a shower of sparks.

A strong vibration began to shimmy throughout Parker's wakemaker as an acrid smell of burning circuits lofted about the cockpit. He looked over at an instrument flag and confirmed his suspicion that a propeller had broken off from his spinner.

Parker radioed, "Rex, I just lost a blade on my secondary."

"Shut it down," Rex's voice crackled back.

"Feathering one."

With a flick of a switch, the first set of propellers ceased spinning and decelerated Parker out of the lead.

"I can't keep up, Rex. You're going to have to take the point," Parker ordered. "Stay in the slot and proceed on course to the next marker, eight points out."

"Understood," Rex confirmed as he passed alongside.

Another wave of anti-aircraft fire flashed ahead as Rex bobbed his wakemaker swiftly into range. He lined the target into his crosshairs and waited to engage the cannons. With a quick pull on the trigger, he managed to knock the support brackets off the enemy installation. As the platform buckled, he watched with high hopes that it would finally topple over.

"Damn it! I blew the pants off that zipper," Rex reported, "but the tower still got boots!"

"Don't worry. I'll get it. Make the turn and head for the last checkpoint."

A deathly groan echoed through Parker's cockpit as his main turbine ground to a halt.

"What was that?"

"I'm losing pressure!"

"Hang in there. I'll swing around and pick you up."

"Negative! Stay on course. The group will be here any minute."

"Toss the kite!"

"Don't worry about me. Just make sure you hit that last target! That's an order."

"I'm not leaving you behind!"

"Pop a cork for me, Rex. Don't forget to check your six," Parker's message fizzled.

Parker grabbed the satchel of gear and unlatched one of the machine guns from its mount. Holding the barrel close to his chest, he angled the crippled wakemaker toward the tower's damaged base.

"No, wait!" Rex shouted.

His message went unheard, as Parker had already ejected.

Floating to the ground, Parker caught sight of his crippled bomber colliding into the base of the enemy tower and erupting in a volcanic shower of molten metal.

Rex looked through his side window and saw the plume of smoke rising in the distance with no indication of a parachute.

"Parker!" Rex cried out, believing his friend to be dead.

With wild-eyed determination, Rex turned his attention back to the final target and lined up for an attack. Pulling on the release handle, he plunged his bombs into the tanks of a fuel depot. The pressurized gas exploded in a ball of flame that hurled his pod forward. He looked back through the cloud of smoke for any signs of a chute or a beacon but saw nothing. Out of ammunition, low on fuel, and with a heavy heart, Rex plotted a return course back to Squeller.

Dangling from a tree and wrapped in a web of cord, Parker detached from his chute and fell to the ground like a sack of potatoes. Luckily for him, he was only a few meters off the ground, and the rain-drenched soil was soft enough to prevent aggravating his still swollen ankle.

A thick layer of smoke from the demolished tower drifted across the ground. Parker rounded up his supplies and trekked into the wilderness ahead. A steady rain tapped off the visor of his helmet and trickled into his eyes. From under the cover of a tall tree, he took a moment to gather his bearings.

He spotted the prison camp down in the valley below and pulled out his old work specs with a telescopic lens to focus in on the facility. The image was fuzzy and speckled with grit, but he could see what appeared to be a group of prisoners being forced out onto the prison grounds.

As he scanned for a suitable place to enter the complex, Parker heard footsteps approaching from the bushes behind him. He spun around and blocked the sharpened mechanical blades of a sentinel with the barrel of the machine gun. The mech continued to press forward, making swift strikes and slashes. Parker managed to evade the onslaught but was soon overpowered by the sentinel's weight and strength. The armored beast loomed over him, lifting its arms high in the air before stabbing down with a mighty blow. Parker parried the attack with the rifle and countered with a succession of rounds blasting into the sentinel's belly. While the armored robot staggered, he armed a small detonator and thrust it into the open wound. Covering his head, he dove to the ground and waited for the grenade to explode. There was a muffled thud that was followed by a puff of white gas. The sentinel wobbled unsteadily before collapsing in a heap of grinding gears.

Out of breath, Parker counted his blessings and did a brief check to make sure that he was still in one piece. He looked at his chronometer and estimated there were only a few minutes left before the second wave of bombers would arrive to destroy what remained of the factory.

Approaching the outer perimeter, Parker noticed Jumbo's body strung up in the center of the compound swaying lifeless in the breeze. He turned away in revulsion. His body began to tremble with rage and his mind became consumed by vengeance. However, when he turned back to see the body for a second time, a deep sense of sorrow and guilt tempered his anger.

Parker crawled along the ground until he came across a break in the fence line and slipped his way onto the prison grounds. Rushing over to the center of the courtyard, he cut down Jumbo's body and held him in his arms.

"I'm sorry, Jumbo," Parker whispered sadly. "I was wrong about you. You came back for me. You saved my life."

As he lowered the lids over Jumbo's eyes, bullets ricocheted off the flagpole behind his head. He looked up and saw a pair of guards rushing toward him firing their side arms. He retaliated with a burst from the machine gun and dove behind a mound of rubble. The wail of an air raid siren began to bellow as crossfire flew in from multiple directions. Realizing that he was being surrounded, Parker took careful aim and fanned a wave of darts across the approaching troops. With the odds mounting against him and time running short, Parker made a last desperate effort to find his sister.

"Kiki! Kiki! Where are you?" he shouted desperately.

Parker felt his heart sink as a final stream of darts blasted out of the barrel. "I'm sorry, Pop," he wept. "I guess my best wasn't good enough."

Tossing the gun to the ground, he heard the rhythmic clang of a coded signal. Tink, tink, tink. The series of taps repeated.

"Kiki?"

Parker surveyed the grounds and estimated that the sounds were coming from a set of concrete chambers buried in the center of the compound. He ran over and dove into a narrow stairwell that ended in a basement doorway. Lifting the heavy rocker of a deadbolt lock, Parker pulled open the rusty door. In the damp cellar, he was shocked to see the pitiful sight of his sister staring back at him. She was thin, wet, and ghostly white. She smiled at him with a weary grin and stared blankly as if she was in a dream. She reached out and gently touched her brother's face.

"Parker? Is it really you?"

"Yes."

Tears flowed as the siblings were reunited. Parker looked down and discovered the intravenous relay attached to Kiki's wrist had been severed. He twisted together a set of wires and patched the circuit with a makeshift jumper before injecting her with a stimulant.

Waiting for the drugs to take effect, he warmed her hands and explained, "Kiki, we have to get out of here. Can you walk?"

"I think so, but –"

"–No buts about it," Parker interrupted. "We gotta go."

Grabbing her hand, Parker checked around the corner before guided her up the stairway.

Ahead of Parker, a squad of sentinels spotted him coming up the stairwell and lowered their bayonets and gun barrels at him. Parker ushered Kiki behind and positioned himself as a human shield. Standing defiantly, he vowed to have his life end with dignity and conviction.

The low drone of approaching aircrafts eclipsed the wail of the air raid siren. The sentinels shifted their attention upward to the wave of bombers approaching over the horizon. Parker squatted down and wrapped his arms around Kiki as the formation of wakemakers soared overhead. Streams of cannon fire strafed across the compound in a hailstorm of destruction and blasted apart the line of mechs.

Chaos ensued as both workers and prisoners raced to take cover. A massive detonation erupted from the factory's core, sending tremors rocketing through the surface. Those closest to the explosion were killed instantly, blown to smithereens, while those farther away were left wandering, disoriented and confused.

Even Parker, who was below ground level, could feel the heat from the blast as it flashed overhead. Through the smoke, he noticed several prisoners dragging themselves along the ground near the main gate, their legs destroyed by the hobblers cuffed around their ankles. He glanced down at Kiki's feet and saw the same insidious devices anchored above her boots.

"Nuts," Parker muttered.

"Like I was trying to tell you," Kiki explained. "They have us wired up pretty good."

Parker pulled an electro-stethoscope out from the satchel and listened for the unit's electric pulse. It was difficult to pinpoint the exact frequency the enemy was using. Back in the day, when he worked as a radioman, Parker was a whiz at fixing towers and deciphering code. He could tune an entire sector with his eyes closed. But this was different. His sister's life was on the line, and the hardware he was tinkering with was foreign and unfamiliar. He narrowed the bandwidth and listened through the series of clicks and squeals. Finally, he came across a tone that sounded about right. He couldn't be sure if it was the correct one, but there were few options left and he had to take a calculated risk. Running a decryption sequence through a buffer, he waited for the moment of truth.

"Here we go, Keek."

Closing his eyes, Parker cut the main lead and Kiki flinched when she heard the snap. Parker peeked back down and saw that the rhythm of the hobbler had successfully been deactivated. Wiping the sweat from his forehead, he turned his attention to the other anklet.

Again, he listened for a signal. Dialing in on the correct modulation, Parker suddenly felt a cold and dreadful aura touch him from afar. He looked up and spotted a figure positioned above in a guard tower, leveling the barrel of a rifle in his direction. Parker could not make out the exact details of the man's face, but he knew exactly whom it was.

That haunting dream, etched in his memory since childhood, was now vividly playing itself out before him. There was a flash, and Parker felt the heat of a searing bullet as it sliced a gash under his eye and tore the stethoscope in two. The ooze of warm blood trickled down his cheek, and for a moment he thought he was dead. It wasn't until he felt the touch of Kiki's cold fingers gripping him tightly that Parker realized he was still very much alive. The mangled stethoscope wisped acrid fumes as it sizzled and fell to the ground. Deep within his mind, Parker knew his destiny was somehow interwoven with the man in the tower but that it would somehow unfold in a distant future. A cloud of thick smoke drifted across Parker's line of sight, and along with the vapor, the man vanished.

Parker grabbed Kiki's hand and pulled her close. He wasn't sure if the second hobbler had successfully been deactivated or not, but there was only one-way to find out.

The two dashed toward the main gate and ran through the perimeter and out of the camp. Passing the last line of fences, Parker could barely contain the elation he felt. Freedom was theirs, if only for a moment. He scanned the area ahead and, with Kiki in tow, ran toward the forest for cover. As they neared the edge of the tree line, the sound of a detonator clinked, and the hobbler strapped around Kiki's ankle exploded. She collapsed to the ground in agony, her foot dangling in a pool of blood.

"Parker!" she cried.

Scurrying back, Parker lifted Kiki into his arms and rushed into the woods. It was a desperate struggle for him to stay ahead of the guards and maintain his footing along the slippery track.

Eventually, they came across a clearing, and Parker rested Kiki against the trunk of a fallen tree. Tearing a piece of cloth from his pant leg, he prepared a makeshift bandage for the open wound. He warned his sister, "This is going to hurt."

Blood squished from the saturated fabric as he pulled the tourniquet tight. Kiki dug her fingers deep in the soil trying not to scream. The ordeal over, she fell back against the stump exhausted.

"Parker," she whispered, "I can't go anymore. My leg, it's no good."

"Just stay focused, Keek. It's going to be okay."

"It hurts too much. I can't move, and I'll just slow you down."

"Don't talk like that. Do you hear me? We're getting out of here. Both of us."

Parker lifted a blood-soaked hand to his face and, like his father before, wiped a single crimson line across his cheeks and nose. As the guards closed in from behind, he pulled the set of hoppers from his sack and snapped them to the bottom of his boots. He hoisted Kiki onto his back and clasped her arms around his neck. As the pneumatic pistons strained under the added weight, Parker shifted to balance the added load. With heavy labor, he began trotting up the incline and did his best to navigate through the wilderness of densely packed trees.

A glow of light illuminated just ahead, and soon they came to the edge of a deep ravine that was spanned by a planked suspension bridge. Parker caught sight of a supply depot and small airstrip covered in camouflaged netting in the gully below. At the other end of the bridge, a single sentinel stood watch near a stairwell that led to the bottom. With the guards approaching from the rear, Parker assessed that their best opportunity to escape was to attack the sentinel head-on. He pulled out a can of smoke and an old chuck. Popping the lid, he tossed the canister ahead as a deterrent.

The sentinel's proximity alert detected the canister and immediately sprung to attention.

Galloping forward into the billowing cloud, Parker lassoed the magnetic karabiner around the leg of the robot and pulled the wire taut. The sentinel staggered as it began blasting holes through the bridge's wooden planks. He pulled again repeatedly, harder until the armored beast finally lost balance and tumbled headlong over the side. Steadfast in its determination to kill, the sentinel fired wildly as it dangled upside down, its body precariously wrapped in the twisted cabling of the handrail.

Guards from the rear positioned themselves along the ravine's edge and took aim. Caught between the crossfire and with nowhere to go, Parker flopped onto his belly and felt the crushing weight of Kiki's body land on top of him. Through the planks, he spotted the flailing robot swaying underneath and noticed a docked transport tucked away in the corner of the depot. In a last-ditch effort, he pulled the pin from a detonator and lobbed it toward the far end of the bridge.

The grenade exploded and sheared the already weakened support. The bridge bucked violently as the cables snapped and plunged them down to the valley below. Parker grabbed hold of Kiki and positioned the pair of hoppers beneath them as he braced for a bone crushing impact.

Looking down, he saw the sentinel's metal casing smash into the ground. A wave of electricity rushed through Parker as the tips of his hoppers made contact with the robot's imploded exoskeleton and could hear the seals on the hopper's gas canisters rupture and the tensioned springs snap under the immense pressure. But to his surprise, the mighty stilts provided just enough cushion to allow him and his sister to survive the fall relatively unscathed.

Snapping his boots free, he dragged Kiki over to the transport and pulled down the lever on the hydraulic entry.

"Come on, you piece of garbage!" Parker leaned his weight onto the door to make it move faster.

The hatch finally lowered, he hoisted Kiki inside and rushed forward into the cockpit. He took a seat in the pilot's chair and examined the unfamiliar control panel. As he tried to decipher the instrument layout, dull echoes of bullets could be heard plinking off the transport's fuselage.

From memory, he talked himself through a basic start up procedure. "Okay. Power, fuel, primer, throttle… Where's the starter?"

Parker scrambled to locate an ignition switch.

"Come on!" Parker panicked. "Where's the damn lighter?"

"Left side, green," Kiki said faintly.

Locating the pair of buttons hidden under safety catches, Parker flipped up the covers and pressed them simultaneously. A blast of compressed air ignited the pulsejet engines and created a horrendous buzz. Pulling on the catapult release, the aircraft jolted forward and began accelerating quickly. Gently, Parker pulled back on the yoke and felt the transport lift into the sky. Once fully airborne, he turned a course for home and looked back at the devastation below.

"So much violence," he whispered sadly. "So much pain."

As the camp disappeared from sight, Parker said farewell to his childhood friend one last time, "Goodbye, Jumbo."

Skimming just above the water, Parker made every effort to avoid coastal detection from Leialil's defense network. He reasoned their best chance to make it back safely was to fly low and hope that no fighters, enemy or otherwise, would spot them.

It wasn't long before Parker became accustomed to the nuances of the transport's flight controls. He took a second to look over his shoulder and spotted Kiki huddling at the rear of the cargo hold. Her face was turning gray and Parker knew if she succumbed to her desire to sleep, she would never again awaken.

"Kiki! Wake up! Don't fall asleep!"

"I'm so tired."

"I know. Just hold on a little longer. Please, you can do it! We're almost there. We're almost home."

"Home," Kiki repeated as she struggled to keep her eyes open.

Trying to pique his sister's interest, Parker shouted over the roar of the engines, "Say, did you hear the news? I got married."

"What? Married?" Kiki perked up. "When?"

"About six months back. It was on a whim. I didn't have time to send you a snip."

"Who cares about that? What I want to know is, 'who did you have to hit on the head to make it happen?'"

"Very funny," Parker replied. "Actually, you're not going to believe it when I tell you."

"Who?" Kiki asked impatiently.

"Well, you remember Tilly?"

"Of course. How could I forget?"

"Well, there you go."

Kiki giggled, "Why, you cheeky charmer, after all these years, you finally bagged the big one. How in the world did you ever manage that?

"Well, to be completely honest, I didn't really do anything. Not really. I mean she's the one who sort of found me."

"That figures," Kiki rolled her eyes. "Leave it up to a woman to do a man's job. Brother, you're hopeless." She smiled, "I guess that makes us sisters now."

"Yeah, I suppose it does," Parker said somberly when he remembered that Tilly was gone.

"It sure would be nice to see her again. I wonder what she's like?"

"Don't worry, you'll have plenty of time to get reacquainted." Parker encouraged. "Just keep your eyes open."

The mood back at Squeller was cheerful as pilots and ground crew alike celebrated the first successful large-scale attack against the Crinch in years. Rex, however, did not partake in any of the festivities. All he wanted to do was to get drunk and be left alone. His heart weighed heavily, for, as far as he knew, his best friend was dead. He looked out at the empty umbilical located outside Parker's cubby.

He raised a bottle and toasted, "Here's to you, bud." Taking a deep gulp and with a stiff upper lip, Rex entered Parker's vacant quarters.

He flipped on the small desk lamp and spotted a few photos mixed in amongst scattered notes and papers. He lifted one up to the light and saw that it was a snapshot taken shortly after graduation of the two friends standing side by side, smiling and brandishing their newly awarded wings.

"Happy days," Rex sighed.

He took a seat at the edge of Parker's bunk and whispered to himself, "I really thought we were gonna beat it."

He polished off the bottle with a final swill before lowering his head onto the desk and listening to the faint echoes of exuberant pilots singing drunk outside. Rex wished he could be like them, sharing stories of peril in the company of friends. But he was alone, the last of his class, and in a twisted and bitter way wanted to keep it that way. He slapped the bottle angrily across the desk and with a hardened scowl exited the dugout.

Wandering the flight deck aimlessly, Rex eventually entered the complex. Through the catacombs of corridors, he passed by the command center and overheard an operator relaying information on an inbound intruder.

"Excuse me, Ma'am. But I think I've got one," the sonar technician reported.

The dispatcher walked over and leaned in on the display, "Where?"

"Three-nine-one, heading southwest."

"Get a fix."

"I can't get a lock. It's coming in too low."

"Probably a floating recon or a skimmer. What's the last contact?"

"Off the coast near the Hipper Flats, K four-one-one."

A garbled message fuzzed in.

"Hold on, there's something else coming through." The operator tuned in and tried to make out the choppy transmission. He channeled the signal through an overhead speaker and flipped it on.

A faint voice hissed. "Midland... This is Har... Vect... Five points off the Hip..." the static transmission fizzled.

"Clean it up," the dispatcher ordered.

"I'm sorry, Ma'am. I can't do any better. All the birds out there are clipped."

The dispatcher scratched her head and contemplated the next course of action. She couldn't be sure if this contact was friendly or not, but protocol dictated that she not take any chances. Opting on a defensive posture, she ordered, "Okay, ring the bell."

"No, wait!" Rex interrupted and grabbed the operator's wrist just before he could punch the alarm. "Play it back again."

The operator obliged.

Rex listened intensely. He couldn't be sure, but something inside him told him to follow his intuition. He turned to the dispatcher and exclaimed, "That's my friend out there! He's coming home!"

"But there's no tag or ticket."

"Trust me," Rex said. "It's one of ours. You've got to send a signal and shut down all the Shellies and Slingers in the sector."

"I can't do that," the dispatcher replied.

"Why not?"

"All the lines are broken, the entire sector is running autonomously. Each unit would have to be cut manually, on site."

"Well, isn't there anyone who can –"

"–Hold on," the dispatcher interrupted. She quickly ran through a set of files on an overhead display and signaled the operator to copy a series of codes. "Post this override and contact the CO. Get a hold of Midland and tell them to ping an emergency broadcast. Notify all the RTOs and tinkers in the sector to terminate the acquisition modules on any active batteries."

"Yes, Ma'am."

"And alert Scoops that we might have a pickup."

Lowering her glasses, she asked Rex once more, "You're sure this thing is friendly?"

"I bet my life on it," Rex nodded firmly.

Streams of light broke through the clouds of a passing storm, and warm rays of late afternoon sun reflected off of Tilly's face as she wrapped up her day's tinkering. Rubbing her firm belly, she gently called out for her old sidekick.

"Smilie, come here. It's time to go home." The ever-jubilant canine lifted his head from the hole he was digging and scampered over to her side.

On a kiosk speaker, a message crackled in. Tilly leaned in to listen, and Smilie suddenly began barking.

"Shh… Smilie, calm down. I can't hear."

But Smilie could not contain himself. He jumped ecstatically and nudged Tilly with intense vigor. She caught only a portion of the message before a low-flying transport suddenly buzzed in over the horizon.

Her heart skipped a beat, as she instinctually knew just who it was that was onboard. "Parker," she mouthed softly.

Low on fuel, the transport's starboard engine began to sputter.

Parker wrestled to stabilize the yawing aircraft as it cruised just above the foothills. He turned to his sister and shouted, "Kiki, we made it!"

Ahead, Parker could see Old Gurdy standing alone, like a beacon amongst the hills of grass. Hope blossomed as the promise of bringing his sister home was now finally coming to fruition. His wish, however, was shattered when a series of explosive rounds pierced through the aircraft's hull and sent the ship plummeting downward. Parker tried to maintain altitude, but a break in the control lines made it impossible. Another blast ripped through the air intake and filled the cabin with smoke. The bulky transport had now been reduced to a burning heap falling from the sky like a flaming meteor.

"Grab something, Keek! We're going down!"

Parker pulled back hard on the yoke and flared on a layer of dense air just before crashing. The heavy undercarriage creaked and rattled as the ship crash-landed and came to a skidding halt.

When the dust finally settled, Parker climbed his way from the cockpit and found Kiki crumpled in a ball. Her lips were blue and her body motionless. He lifted her into his arms and kicked open the rear hatch.

A gust of cool air rushed in, clearing away the smoke. Parker found Old Gurdy standing before him just a stone's throw away. He walked over to the old oak tree and softly rested his sister against the base of the trunk. With the tips of his fingers, he brushed Kiki's hair back and folded it behind her ears. The bandage wrapped around her ankle was dripping with blood and slowly leaking what remained of her precious life's fluid.

"I'm cold," Kiki shivered.

Parker placed Tilly's vest across her chest and dialed up the heating rheostat.

"Here, this will keep you warm," he said while trying to assess the situation.

Parker knew if he left his sister to get help, she would most likely die before his return. But staying with her would only make that a certainty. He weighed his options and decided that his best chance was to make contact with a local outpost and bring back support.

He wiped the tears from his eyes and explained to his sister. "Kiki, I'm going to get help. It's only a few clicks down to Mumpy."

"No, Parker! Please, don't go." Kiki pleaded.

"But you need a medic."

"I don't want a doctor. I just want you to stay here with me."

"But I can save you."

"It's too late for that now."

"Don't talk like that. You're going to be fine. We made it! We're home! You just have to hold on a little longer. Just a little bit more."

"I'm so tired," Kiki murmured.

"No! Don't sleep! Keep your eyes open! He snapped off his pilot's wings and placed them into Kiki's palm. Here, hold these. They'll keep you safe from any rogue mechs." Parker scanned the horizon and determined the shortest route back to civilization. He looked at his sister a final time and said, "I'll be back in a snip."

"Please, Parker. Don't go!"

Her voice went unheard, as Parker was already in full stride and sprinting down the hill.

He ran as fast as he could, faster than he ever had before. Trying desperately to escape the pain of death and the ineffable fear cast in its shadow.

As the cries of his sister faded, Parker focused his attention on reaching the sector outpost located deep within the Mumpy Grove.

With the sun dipping behind a blanket of clouds and the temperature dropping, Parker could feel the joints of his knees and ankles stiffening. Every step down the steep grade sent another jolt of pain shooting through his already burning legs. Having only his flight suit to protect him from the elements, Parker knew he was in trouble, not that he would succumb to the cold but rather that he no longer had any form of identification to protect him from a passing Grazer or Snuff.

Taking a moment to catch his breath, Parker could see the Chatley Ruins just up the next ridge and he told himself, "If I can just make it there unharmed, it's a downhill skip to the grove." Cold air tickled his dry throat, and he cupped his hands over his mouth to warm his hands. Surveying the landscape ahead, he heard the sound of a mechanical motor whizzing through the grass nearby.

Parker immediately stood still and looked for signs of tracks on the ground. A few moments passed before he heard another rustle closing in from behind. Spinning around,

Parker felt the sharp blades of a grazer slice across the backside of his calf. He grunted in pain as his body collapsed to the ground. Quickly, he scurried to find something he could use as a weapon, and luckily came across a fist-sized stone. Listening attentively, he waited for the mech's next move.

Parker heard another rustling in the grass. He held his breath as his senses tingled with anticipation. He knew evading the mech was going to difficult and painful. There was, however, one small chance to defeat it, for like the nimble crustaceans they were designed after, grazers, too, had a vulnerable soft spot beneath their armored shells.

A shimmering blade speared through the brush in front of Parker's face. He lifted his hands to cover his eyes. The piercing dagger impaled through the muscle of his forearm and straight into the bone. Twisting his arm, Parker flipped the robot over to expose its vulnerable ventral side. With a forceful blow, he smashed the rock against the grazer's mechanical innards. Sprockets flew and hydraulic fluid spurted as the fierce little beast convulsed and squealed. Eventually, the thrashing ceased and the damaged robot hung like a wet towel draped over his arm. With an agonizing pull, Parker extracted the twisted blade and tossed the mangled mech to the ground.

Dripping a trail of blood, Parker limped his way over to the Chatley Ruins. He pushed open the remnants of a thick timber door and edged his way inside. Portions of the collapsed ceiling formed a carpet of rubble that lay scattered across the floor. Shafts of light filtered through the windows, creating glittering pools that lit the great cathedral in a soft glow.

At the center of the room, Parker took a seat against a collapsed column. He pulled out the snapshot of Kiki outfitted as a radioman and stared at it in tearful remembrance. Parker knew that Kiki would not survive, but he did not have the courage to be with her during her final moments when death would come and he would again be left alone.

Parker crumpled the picture into a ball and tossed it to the ground. He couldn't help but wonder why so much cruelty had befallen him and why he had to suffer. He screamed at the top of his lungs, but it was an empty roar. When the echoes of his voice subsided, all that remained were the distant memories of family and friends, and the void left behind, marking the passage of their once vibrant lives.

Unable to reconcile the grief he felt, Parker sat in denial. Perhaps the pain was too great, or maybe he was simply unwilling to accept it. Whatever the case, because of that single flaw – all he had left – all he could do, was run.

Parker dusted off his pants and limped his way to a nearby window. He scanned for any signs of danger still lurking in the tall grass. Over the crest of the next hill, he could see the tops of the trees that lined the Mumpy Grove.

"Five minutes," he told himself. "I'll be there in five minutes."

Parker narrowed his focus and hopped down from the ledge. The foot inside his blood-soaked boot squished, leaving a gruesome imprint along the crusted ground. He wiped the perspiration from his brow and quickly filled his lungs with oxygen before making a dash from the ruins.

Hobbling as fast as he could, Parker could smell the faint wisps of spring blossoming cottonwood and lavender filling the air ahead, signaling he was getting close.

"Almost there," he said. "Just one more minute!"

Nearing the stronghold, Parker tried to recall some of his old passwords that might allow him access into the underground complex. As he searched his memory, a sudden shrill surged like a whistling kettle and broke his concentration. He looked up and spotted a puck-shaped canister floating upward ahead of him and spinning like a top. Parker covered his ears and closed his eyes as the suicidal snuff blew itself apart into a thousand bits.

When Parker came to, he felt no pain. Nor did he feel cold or hungry. Everything was in order and serene. The only evidence of any previous drama was a small crater smoldering at his feet. The world outside was silent, and the air was calm and warm.

Ahead of him, a silhouetted figure waved enthusiastically. Parker didn't know if what he saw was real, but his heart was filled with joy as he called out, "Jumbo!"

He charged up the hill as the image sharpened – the man waving at him was indeed his old friend. He raced forward; wanting to apologize for all that had happened and let Jumbo know how much he admired his leadership and courage. But just as he came within range, Parker slipped on a loose patch of dirt and stumbled headlong into the grass.

Struggling to regain his footing, a dark shadow loomed overhead. Parker looked up and saw the piercing eyes of the Griffin staring back at him. The awe-inspiring beast with its huge talons and a hooked mandible gently cupped Parker against its feathery plumage and encapsulated him. With a wave of its powerful wing, Parker was transported to another place and time.

Appearing back at the entrance of the cell that once imprisoned his sister, the Griffin guided Parker down the stairwell and waited as he cautiously peeked through the open door.

The room inside was dark and damp, and it took some time for Parker's eyes to adjust. A sickly smell of mold and mildew lingered heavily in the cool stagnant air. At the far end of the room dangled a small overhead lamp. He could just make out the vague outline of someone lying prone, bound in restraints along the smooth metal surface of a mechanical rack. Sounds of water droplets echoed throughout the concrete chamber. Parker could feel the presence of another moving just beyond the periphery. He stood quietly as he watched a frail hunched old man in a white laboratory coat lumber into the glow of the light with a prepared syringe in his hand.

The patient strapped along the rack also sensed someone entering the doorway and shifted his eyes to see who it was. There was a sudden pinch in his forearm, and Parker felt the warming of an injection flowing up through his veins. For a moment, Parker did not know if he was the man in the doorway or the man on the table. A strange dizziness muddled his thoughts, and he found it difficult to concentrate. A blurred image crossed his vision when he narrowed his eyes to focus. He saw the Doc's decrepit face slowly sharpened into view. At first it startled him. But soon he found comfort in seeing the old man's familiar gaze.

Parker's memory drifted back to the hills, and he called out, "Jumbo, where are you?"

The Doc reached for the handle of a large crank-arm with his muscular hand. "Please do not move," he politely advised.

"What have you done with him?" Parker asked.

The Doc did not respond until after making a final check on the straps binding Parker's hands and feet. "Just lie still," he said.

Frightened, Parker struggled to escape from the restraints.

"What are you doing?" he asked anxiously. "Who are you? Where am I?"

"At the threshold," the Doc replied.

"Threshold?"

"You are on the cusp, caught within the twilight world that separates the living from the dead. You are here to make a choice, and I am here to help guide you to the truth."

"The truth?" Parker asked. "What truth?"

"The truth of why you suffer," answered the Doc.

"What suffering? I don't have time for this. I have to get back. Jumbo, I saw him. He's alive! And my sister…" Parker's thoughts scattered, and he became agitated. "I have to find help. She needs me. I can save her. Please, I promised I would take care of her!"

With a turn of the winch, Parker's limbs were pulled taut.

"Unfortunately, that time has passed."

"Please!" Parker pleaded. "I can do it! I can make it happen. I can bring her back. I can bring them all back."

The Doc's arm heaved another revolution. Parker's joints burned as his muscles and tendons began to stretch.

"Why did you leave her?" the Doc asked.

"I didn't. I didn't leave her. I needed to get help."

Kiki's last words echoed through the chamber: "Please, Parker. Don't go!"

Parker writhed defiantly, trying to shut out the traumatic plea.

"Why did you let her die alone?"

"I didn't. Don't you see? You've got it all wrong!" Parker shouted. "I couldn't stay. I needed to get help!"

"And your father? Why did you leave him?"

"I didn't —"

The rack pulled tighter until the straps binding his wrists and ankles began tearing into his flesh.

"Stop! Please!" He broke down in tears. "Can't you understand? I had to leave. It was too hard. I couldn't..."

"Watch him die?"

"Yes. But I can save my sister."

"How? She has already passed."

"No!" Parker vehemently denied. "I don't believe you! You're lying!"

In the far corner of the room, the lifeless body of Kiki's corpse illuminated. Her arms wrapped around her knees, she lay cradled like a fetus in the womb.

"Kiki!" Parker screamed in horror.

Another cog clicked, and the rack pulled tighter. Parker tried to fight the pain, but it was his refusal to accept the truth that prolonged the torture. Two more bodies came into view, and he could see the faces of his father and Jumbo staring back at him hauntingly with watchful eyes.

Parker cried out, "Please, stop!"

An eerie pop sounded as the joints of his limbs began to separate.

Sweat poured down Parker's face.

"Why are you doing this?"

"It is not me," said the Doc. "It is your own memory that haunts you. Hope has turned to despair, expectation to disappointment."

"That's not true! It's you! You're the one doing this! I hate you!" Parker screamed.

"The burdens of the past weigh heavily over time," the Doc explained. "Until they become unbearable and must be laid to rest."

"But I can't!" Parker cried. "I won't!"

The Doc's muscular arm heaved another cog in the rack's pulley. "It is attachment that keeps you bound, and your unwillingness to change that causes you pain."

"Please, no more!" Parker conceded. "I'll do anything. Just stop the pain!"

Spotting the Griffin resting in the shadows, Parker mouthed a desperate plea.

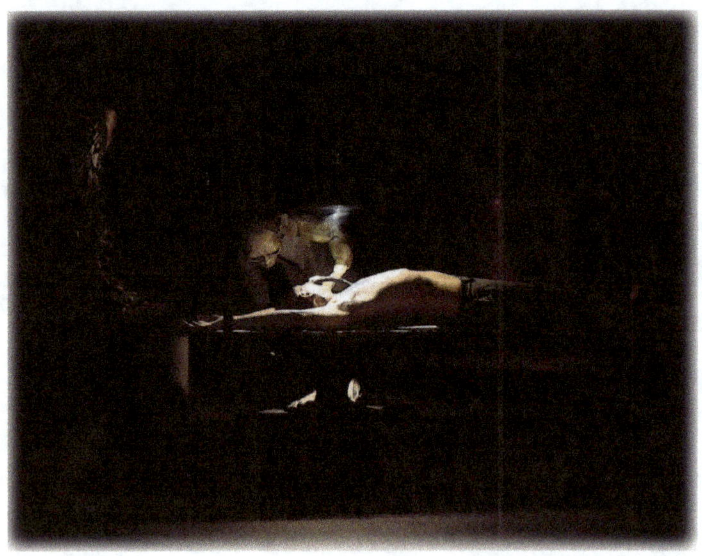

The great beast rose from the ground and neared. Leaning in, the Griffin placed its hawkish beak sharply against Parker's throat. Parker could feel the deep exhalation from the Griffin's powerful lungs blowing wisps of warm breath across his face as he prepared himself for death.

The Griffin gazed upon him with piercing eyes. Parker stared back, his heart filled with fear. As he waited for the end to come, Parker could feel a calmness emanating from the creature's spirit, a strength and kindness that reminded him of his father.

Another painful jolt stretched Parker to an arresting height, and he shivered in terror as his body was on the verge of being torn apart.

"Help me," Parker wept.

The Griffin acknowledged Parker's woeful plight and, with a wave of his wing, whisked him to a final realm.

In an instant, Parker found himself standing amongst the hills of his home, waist deep in swaying grass and under a warm summer's glow. All the pain had vanished and the lush glen of Slipper's Pass bloomed just ahead. The Griffin remained silent as Parker made his way down to the trickling creek that snaked its way through the trees.

At the edge of the stream, he spooned a finger of soft mud and reminisced about the days gone by. As he smoothed the soil between his index finger and thumb, a ghostly apparition faded into view. The luminous figure softly transformed into the body of a young girl and it took a moment for Parker to recognize who it was. He asked curiously, "Kiki?"

The girl smiled. "It's good to see you, Park."

"How did you get here?"

"You brought me here."

Parker couldn't quite comprehend what he was experiencing – a place beyond dreams, yet not entirely real.

He looked around and examined the simple perfection that abounded, from the twinkling rays of sun mirroring off the water, to the gentle aroma of lemongrass and chamomile that danced in the mellow breeze. He sat down at Kiki's side and asked. "What is this place?"

"A memory," Kiki said.

She looked over and examined Parker's face.

"You look like Pop."

Parker did his best to stifle his emotions. "I've missed you, Sneak."

"I know," she replied tenderly.

Kiki reached over and took hold of her brother's hand as they sat along the tranquil shore.

After a while, she turned and said, "Parker. I've come here to say goodbye. But I wanted to thank you for being there when I needed you most and for watching over me all those years."

"But I couldn't save you," Parker said regretfully.

"You tried your best. That's all that matters… I was lucky to have you as my brother. I know it wasn't always easy," she said with a playful grin. "But, hey, it sure was fun. Don't ya think?"

Parker nodded. "I wouldn't have it any other way."

Standing in the background, the Griffin signaled to Kiki that it was time to leave.

"I have to go now."

"Couldn't you stay, just a little while longer?"

"I'm sorry, but it's my time to leave and yours to return."

"Maybe, I could go with you?" Parker asked tearfully.

"Oh, Parker. I know how hard this must seem. But there's still much more left for you to do."

"Please, Kiki. I miss you all so much. I want to go back. I want to feel whole again."

"Sometimes, the only way back is to keep moving forward, step by step, until one day you realize that you're right back where you started."

"But I'm afraid. I don't want to be alone."

"You're not," Kiki said, placing her hand over his heart. "We're all here. You just need to ask for us and remember to listen to the wind. It's all so simple. Life – it's as easy as a fall."

"I wish I could believe that. I wish I could stay here and have this moment last forever."

"Nothing lasts forever," she paused and winked. "It gets better."

"Will I ever see you again?

Kiki giggled. "Does Jumbo wear big pants?"

Parker thought for a moment and smiled.

"Take care, Park."

"See ya, Sneak."

Kiki's body changed back into its translucent state and drifted back into the woods with the Griffin, disappearing from sight.

Stretched along the rack, the Radioman stared blankly into the void. The Doc watched closely as a wave of serenity flowed over his patient. His powerful arm softened, and the tension on the restraints released. The darkness of the chamber dissolved away, replaced by the lush hillside of Kakydurn, where Parker was returned back to the world of the living.

Lying prone in the grass, Parker was unable to move his arms or legs. A sick metallic flavor filled his mouth and he could smell the distinct scent of burnt flesh and cordite floating through the air. His head throbbed and nearly every bone in his body felt rattled out of place.

A passing cloud drifted overhead and he heard the muffled sound of a dog approaching in the distance. The jubilant barking became louder and Parker had a good idea of who it was.

"Smilie?"

Through the grass, the boisterous retriever burst into view and began sniffing Parker's tattered body and licking his wounds.

A voice called out and whistled, "Smilie! Where are you? Did you find him?"

The dog barked affirmatively as his owner neared.

"Tilly?"

"Parker?"

Tilly rushed over and kneeled down next to Parker's side.

"Parker! Is it really you?"

"Yes, it's me. I'm home."

Tilly could sense the severity of injuries suffered by her husband. She gently touched his face. "Just lay still," she cautioned. "Smells like you just lost a bet with a snuff."

Parker gazed longingly at Tilly as she raced to elevate his feet and tie a bandage around his leg.

"You sure are a sight for sore eyes," Parker smiled.

"Well, I'm definitely hard to miss. I'm almost twice the girl that I was when you left."

For the first time, Parker noticed that his wife was pregnant. "Jiggers, Tilly! You're huge!"

"Thanks for noticing. I'll take that as a compliment. You know, you're partially to blame. I know this might come as a bit of a shock to you, but you're about to become a father."

"A what?" Parker was dumbfounded. "I mean, how?"

Tilly chuckled. "I'll explain later."

Securing the bandage, she leaned in and kissed him tenderly.

"I told you I'd come back."

"And so you did," Tilly agreed. "It's nice to know you're a man of your word."

From under the clouds, Rex's wakemaker rumbled overhead and hovered in for a landing.

Parker tried to get up but found his body too broken and exhausted. He looked down and saw a flurry of intravenous tubes and electrodes attached to his arms and torso. He followed the trail of wires with his eyes and spotted a tiny medical mech standing next to him busily tending to his injuries and monitoring his condition.

It soon dawned on him that this little robot with its gleaming spherical head and delicate mechanical arms was responsible for saving his life, and more importantly, his spirit. With deep gratitude, he said, "Thanks, Doc."

The little mech beeped an affirmative chirp as it prepared Parker for transport.

A brilliant canvas of color beamed across the sky, and for the first time in his life, Parker was at peace. Everything he wished for had come together in this fleeting moment in time, and though he knew it ultimately would not last, for the moment at least, he was safe…

Additional

Map of Leialil

Map of Kakydurn

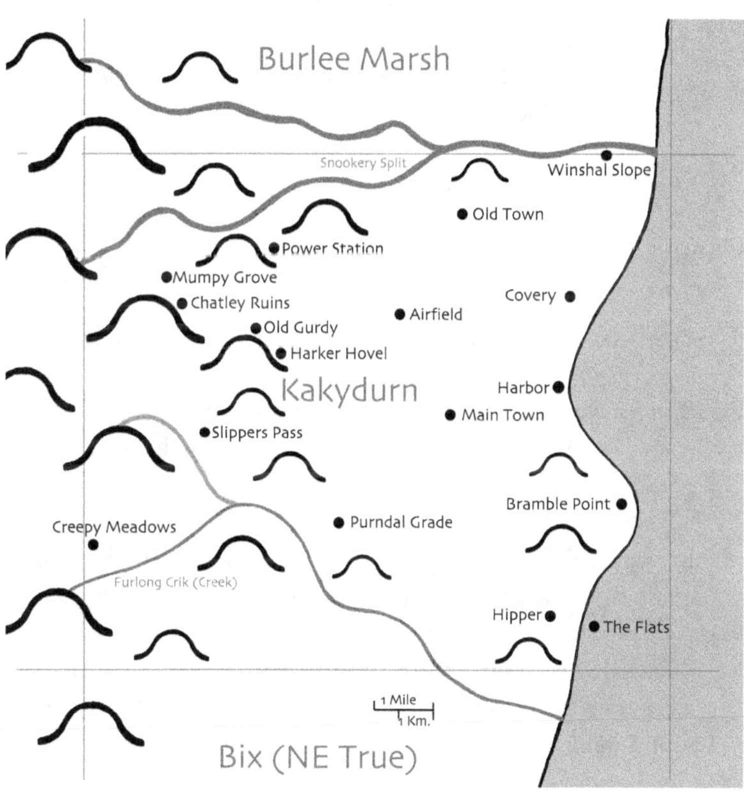

Glossary

Ace – A pilot with 5 or more kills

Air Armory – Leialil's combat air force and a subdivision of the Air Response Ministry.

Air Response Ministry – A government branch in charge of all aerial operations, commonly known as Air Operations (Air Ops) or ARM.

Birdhouse – A sonar array.

Bobber – A life preserver/vest.

Box – An area consisting of 9 grids or 30 square kilometers.

Brill – An alcoholic beverage, clear in color and distilled from various grains or tubers, such as wheat, rice, or potatoes.

Brown Brill – Distilled alcoholic liquor that is amber in color, made from barley and casketed in smoked wooden barrels.

Buzzard – A slang term used to describe a Crinch fighter. The nickname was derived from the distinct "buzzing" sound made by the pulse jet engines.

Cattail – A radio transmission array.

Ceelie Peninsula/Launch – A strip of land located east of Kakydurn and attached to the northeast corner of Bix.

Central – Leialil's military communication branch, divided into prefecture dispatch regions with network information funneled to a central command center.

Charmer – A mystical creature that is humanoid in form but possesses supernatural powers.

Chatley Ruins – An abandoned monastery that was destroyed during the early years of the war.

Chuck – A magnetic attachment (karabiner) used to ascend large-scale superstructures.

Criestruden – An industrialized nation located on the continent of Parlimey. Its roots are based on a caste system of hierarchy and paternal leadership. It values economic wealth and a strong sense of nationalistic pride.

Crinch – A derogatory term used to identify the people of the nation Criestruden.

Daisy Point – A sector defense outpost.

DOD – Damaged or destroyed.

Dink – A general term used to denote a small fastener used to connect electrical connections.

Doc – A medical robot.

Downy – An allied nation to Leialil and located on the continent of Parlimey. Its borders include the entire west coast of the continent. It is also the last major stronghold to prevent Criestruden from western domination.

Drey – A bar or pub.

Duck – 1. A ducted fan (vertical lift) unit. 2. Reference to a ducted fan transport.

Dupe – A radio-jamming beacon.

EDN – Electronic Detection Network that includes: Radio transmission arrays, sonic detectors, anti-aircraft batteries, and anti-infantry installations.

Field Operations – (Field Ops) Military Land/Sea units that include: infantry, technical support, infrastructure, and defense perimeter operations.

Grayvel – A small oily fish packed and steamed in tin containers.

Grazer – A small stealthy mech designed to hobble or otherwise injure intruders. It uses sharp razor-like claws to incapacitate enemy combatants.

Grid – An area of 10 sq. km.

Hoverball Operator (H-Op) – Personnel who can fly vertical-lift transports and navigate using visual flight techniques. This type of pilot is not qualified to operate secondary thrust aircraft or perform instrument navigation, nor trained in combat flying.

Hedgehog – A defensive military installation whose battery of rockets resembles a blanket of quills.

Hopper – Pneumatic powered stilts.

Hoverball – A vertical lift turbine system.

Kakydurn – A village located on the east coast of Leialil. Known for rolling hills and lush grasslands.

Keller – A coastal area located in the upper east region of the Leialil. Known for its sheltered cove and inlet bay.

Kicker – An ejection seat.

Leialil – An island nation roughly 1000 km long and 500 km wide. Named after the rabbit spirit Leialilthethuthenang (Floral Light). The northern region is made up of mountain cliffs and rocky jetties, while the southern regions consist of fertile plains and wetlands.

March – The capital city of Leialil. Located in the upper west region of the country and surrounded by a natural stronghold of steep mountain cliffs. The city consists of a set of arcologies that house the main government ministries and civilian population.

Marigold Line – A defensive perimeter that surrounds the entire mainland of Leialil.

Maver Air Proving Ground – A military pilot training facility.

Mech – A robot with artificial intelligence.

Medic – A first response medical mech that roams assigned routes along the defense perimeter of Leialil.

Motley – Any variety of homemade stew.

Mumpy Grove – A tree lined ravine where Daisy Point Outpost is located.

Persey – A monastery.

Pod – A colloquial term referring to a wakemaker aircraft.

Pounder – A pilot with 10+ kills. Referred to by the number of kills and the added suffix pounder (i.e. 12 kills = A twelve-pounder).

Radioman – A radio/communication technician.

Re-O – A replacement Operator/Officer.

Rover – A military vehicle or a search and rescue unit.

RTO – Radio Technician and Operator.

Sector – An area consisting of 50 sq. km.

SR – Search and Rescue (AKA Scoops).

Sentinel – A Crinch armor-plated soldier or robotic guard.

Sled – A modular storage bunk/bed.

Snip – A recorded audio message.

Snippet – An instant photograph.

Snuff – A robotic mine.

Slewy – A wetland area located along the southern coast of Leialil.

Slinger – An anti-aircraft battery.

Spinner – A propeller driven horizontal propulsion unit.

Squadron – A defensive aerial unit. Made up of intercept fighters and patrol aircraft.

Squeller – A coastal region in the northeast region of Leialil. Known for its rocky jetty that houses an underground airbase.

Strike Group – An offensive aerial unit made up of bombers and accompanying escort, commonly referred to simply as a "Group."

Tag – A military call sign or I.D. Moniker.

Thumper – A field sensor that detects land-based movement.

Tinker – A field operation repairman. Includes: Radio Operators and Mech Service Personnel.

Ticket – A password or sequence code used to verify identification.

Turnpike – An electrical switch/spigot used to redirect current.

Twig - A Treun/Westoleby surveillance mech.

Wakemaker – An aeronautical ship built in modular segments and configured for a variety of missions including: Bombing, Escort, Ground Attack, Intercept, Patrol, Reconnaissance, Transport, and (SR) Search and Rescue.

Ranks

Field Operations – Land and Coast

<u>Enlisted Ranks (Deck Operator)</u>

⌒ - Recruit

⌒ - D.O. I – Operator

⌒ - D.O. II – Technician

⌒ - D.O. III – Specialist

<u>Non-Commissioned Officers</u>

▬ - D.F. – Deck Officer I (Half Bar / Baby Bar shown)

● - Hoverball Operator (H-OP) for
Air Operations within Field Division.
(Minimum rank: D.O. Specialist)

<u>Commissioned Officers</u>

⌒ - Pack Leader

✕ - Field Officer

✕ - Captain (with enlisted marker)

Ⓦ - Warren Officer

✳ - Field Commander or CO

⊗ - Executive Officer XO or Base Commander

⊗ - Field Primary FP (w/enlisted marker)

Air Control (Operations)
Air Armory (Combat) and Air Utility (Support)

<u>Enlisted Ranks – (Air Combatant)</u>

⌒ - Recruit

- A.C. I - Airman

- A.C. II – Technician

- A.C. III – Rigger or Chief

<u>Non-Commissioned Officers</u>

 - D.F. – Deck Officer II (Full Bar shown)

<u>Commissioned Officers</u>

- Pilot Wings

- Ensign (Non-Pilot) or Pilot Officer

- Lt. (Non-Pilot) or Flight Lieutenant

- Captain or Flight Leader

- Breaker/Squadron Leader (w/enlisted marker)

- Air Commander AC or Group Leader

- Air Executive AX (w/enlisted marker)

- Air Primary AP

<u>Confirmed Civilian Staff</u>

Branch Representative (Land)
Wing Primary (Air)

RADIO/·\AN

Class III Ribbons

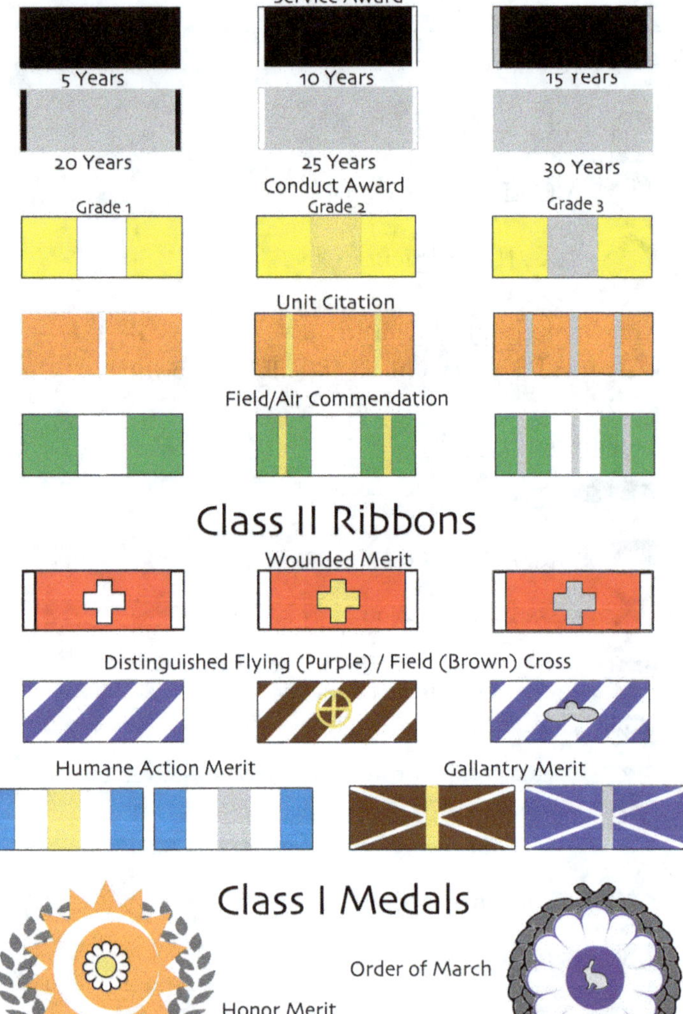

Class II Ribbons

Class I Medals

WAKEMAKER SEGMENTS

Blower Mk.I
Propulsion - Turbine

The "Blower" series vertical lift system is the successor to the "Hoverball" unit. The compact turbine produces a climb rate of 400 m/min., a hover altitude of 5 km, and a horizontal cruising speed of 150 km/hr. Used primarily as the VLS on fighter/bomber configurations.

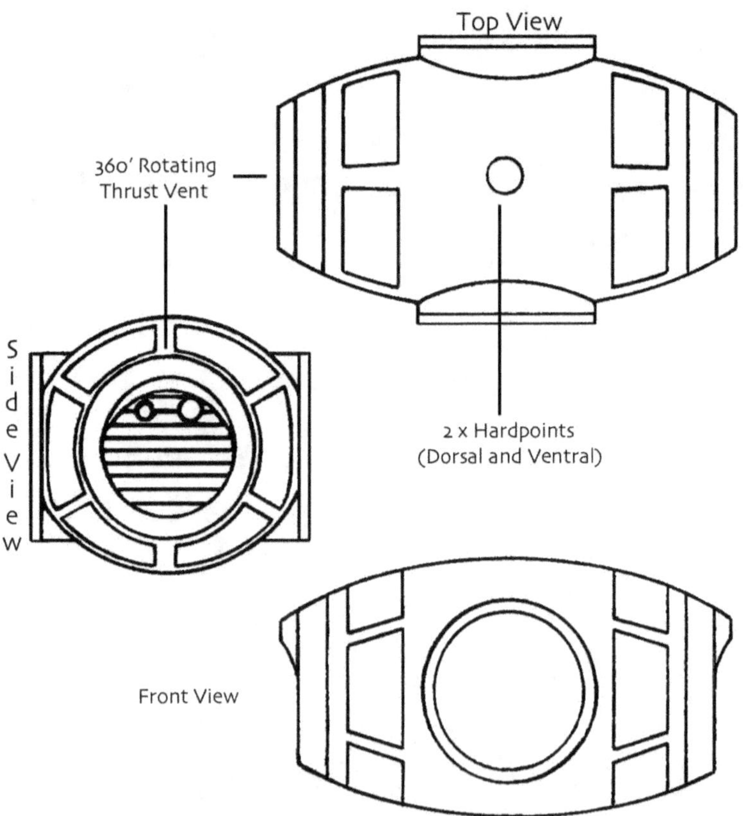

Blower Mk.II
Propulsion - Turbine

Twice as large but with nearly twice the lifting power of the Mk.I "Blower" class vertical lift system. The Mk.II is primarily attached to heavy bombers or freight transports.

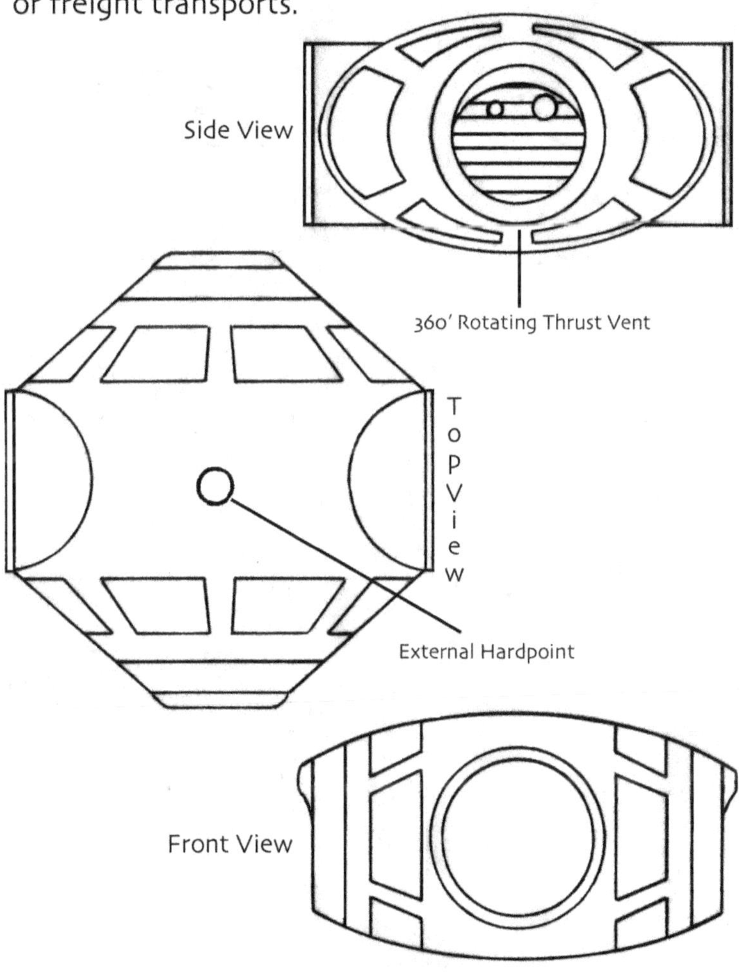

Bomber Pod Mk.I

Crew: 1-Pilot & 1-Gunner

The Bomber Pod seats two crewmen in tandem - a forward facing pilot and a rear facing gunner/sonar operator. It is equipped with 3 multi-purpose auxillary hardpoints and can be reconfigured for fighter or strike detail.

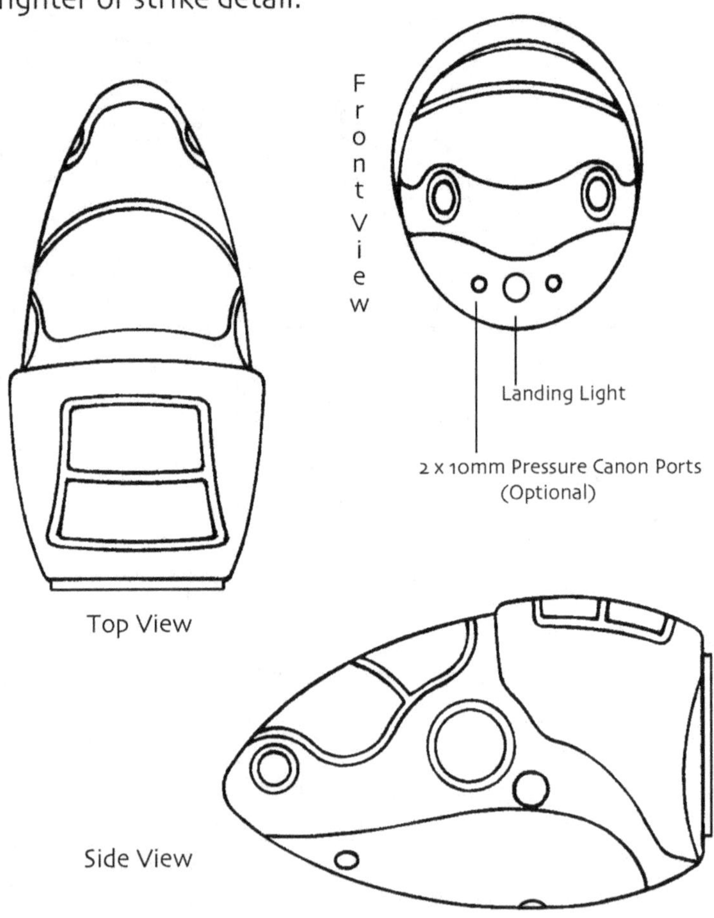

End Cap Mk.I

The tail end segment of a wakemaker. This unit houses 360' radar detection and short range communication equipment. It also contains retractable landing gear, and 3 external hardpoints that can attach UHF long range communication antenna, rocket powered short boost pack(s), or evasive scatter shot.

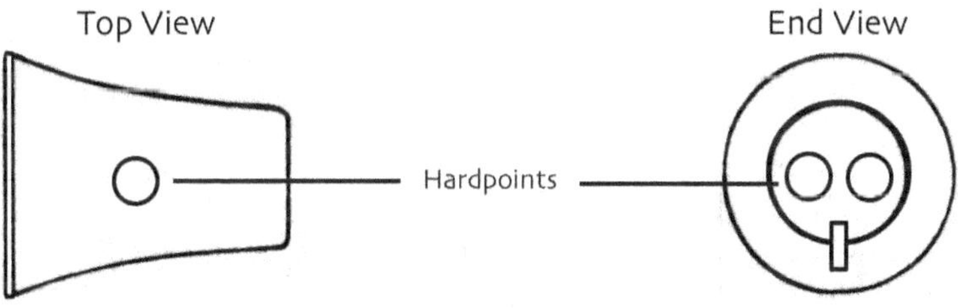

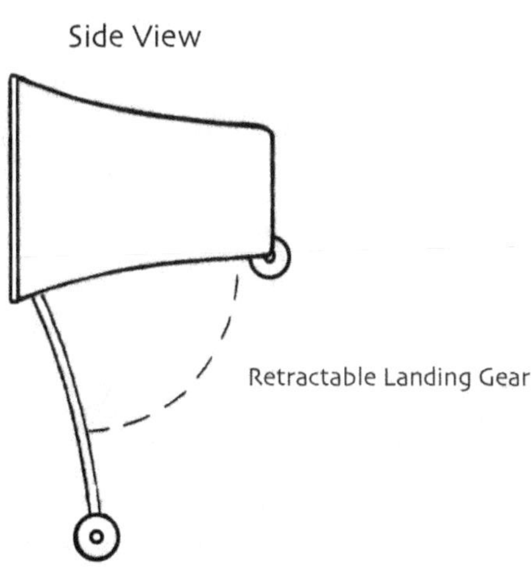

Fighter Pod Mk.I

Crew: 1-Pilot

The single man fighter pod is the basic unit designed for intercept and escort detail. It is equipped with 3 mulit-purpose hardpoints that can attach additional stabilizers, high-caliber (15 or 20mm) pressure canons, rocket launchers, or other sonic/radio hardware.

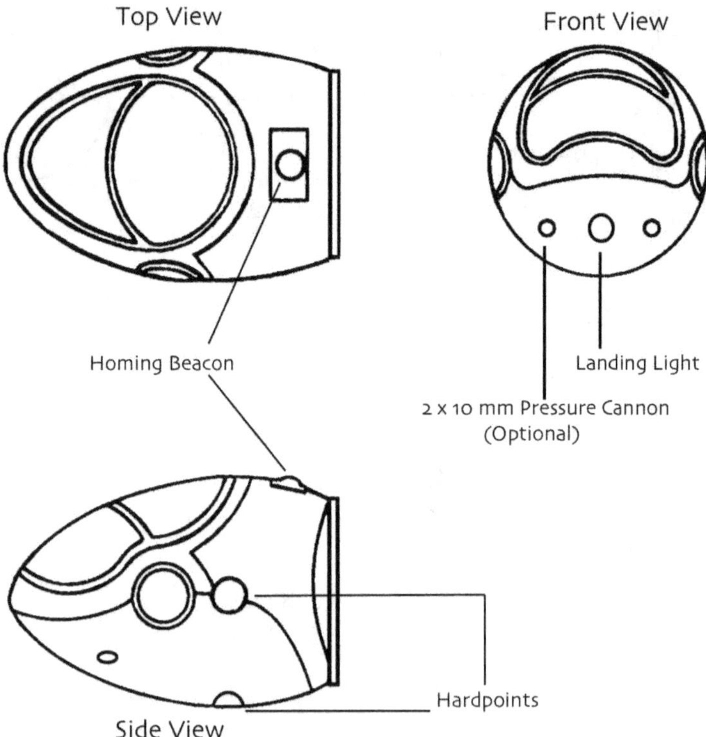

Gun/Bomb Rack Mk.I

The Gun/Bomb rack is an external platform attached to light and medium bombers as well as other strike aircraft. Used for both strafing and aerial engagement, the pod has 6 hardpoints that can affix 10/15/20mm cannons, rocket launchers (explosive, incendiary, marking flares, or smoke), scatter packs, range sonar, or hold 350 kg of bombs. Powered by its own fuel cell and pressure turbine, it stores enough energy to simultaneously fire high caliber cannons and scatter packs until its ammunition is depleted. When outfitted solely with rockets or bombs, the rear mounted turbine can be removed to provide added internal space or an extra 150 kg of bombs.

Side View

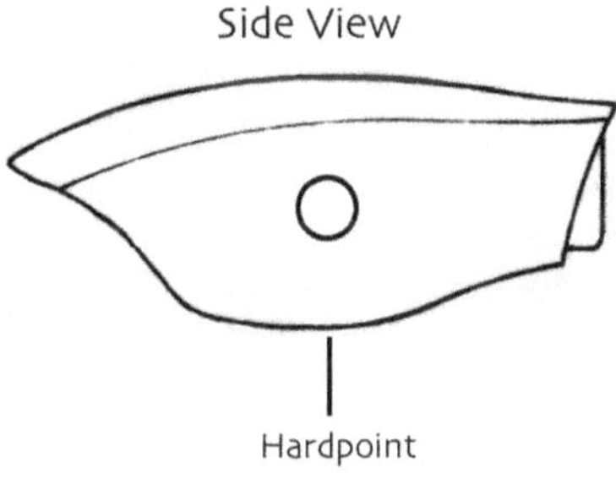

Hardpoint

Front View

Hardpoints

Top View

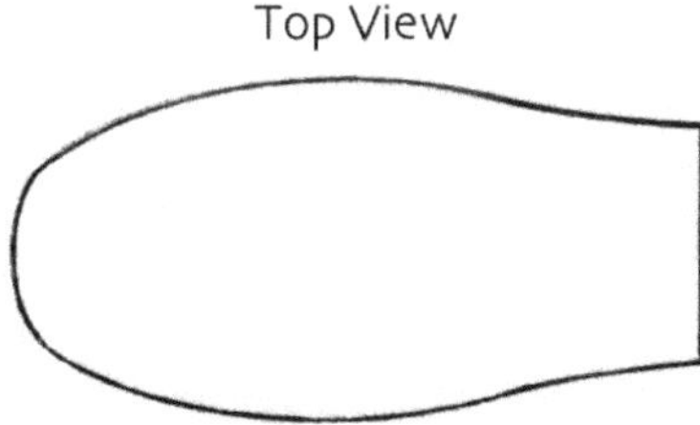

Hoverball - Mk.I
Propulsion - Ducted Turbine

The hoverball provides vertical lift during take-off and descent. The turbine fan unit is contained within a sphere-shaped cowling that can rotate up to 90' in any direction. When additional lift is not needed, the fan unit rolls to a drag-reducing position.

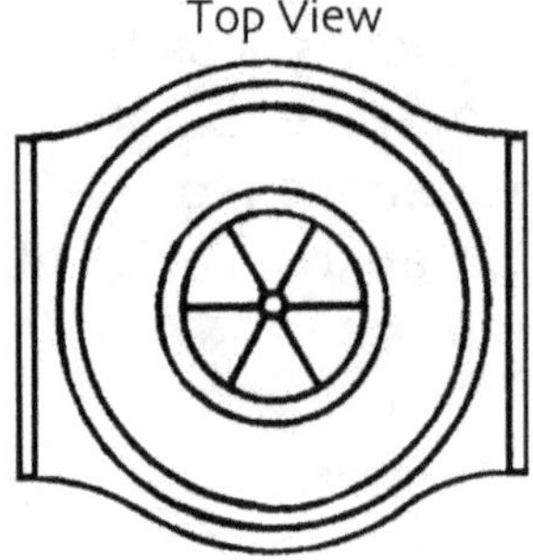

Top View

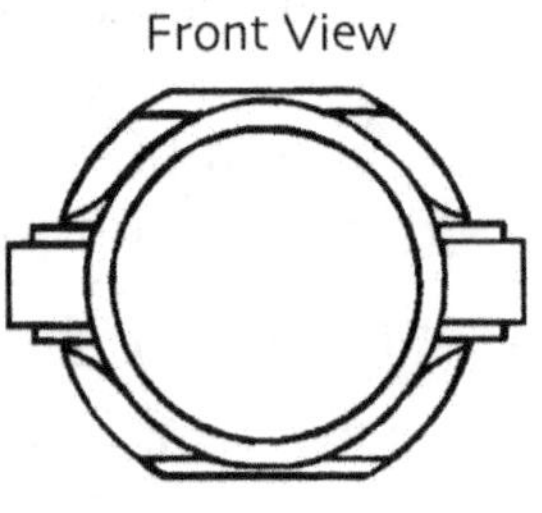

Front View

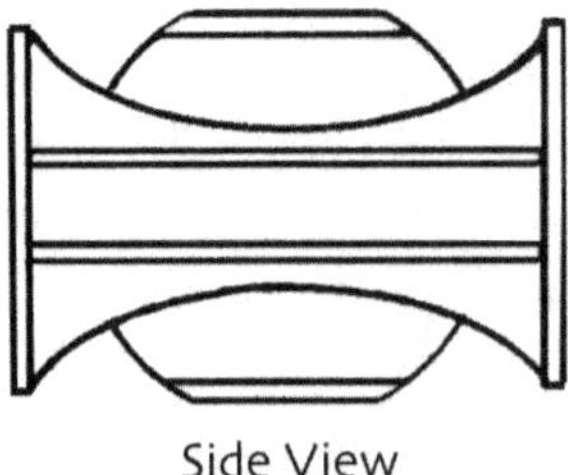

Side View

Reconnaisance Pod Mk.I

Crew: 1 Pilot/Sonar Operator or Autonomous Program

The reconnaisance pod is the first design to support both internal and external hardpoints. It may be configured to support one pilot and various sensors or can be refitted as a mechanized unit with an interchangable cowling that can house 2 internal devices such as additional pressure canons, rocket launchers, or sonar/radar detection equpiment.

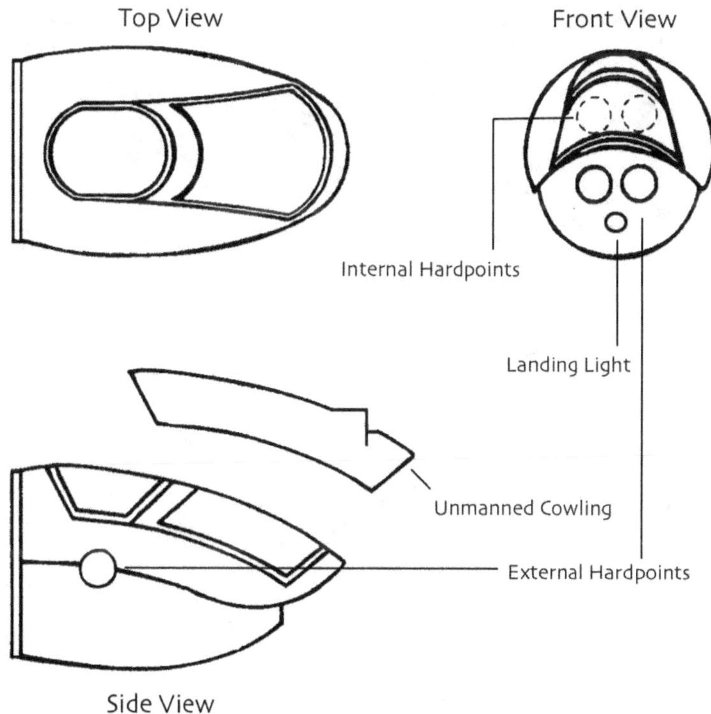

Remote / A.I. Pod

Crew: 0/1-A.I. or Remote Controlled

A concept pod affectionately refered to as the "Porpoise," but more commonly known as a "Dud." This unmanned design utilizes flex-programmable memory for reconnaisance sorties but can also be controlled remotely for use as a short-range fighter/interceptor. Contains 6 internal and 2 external hardpoints.

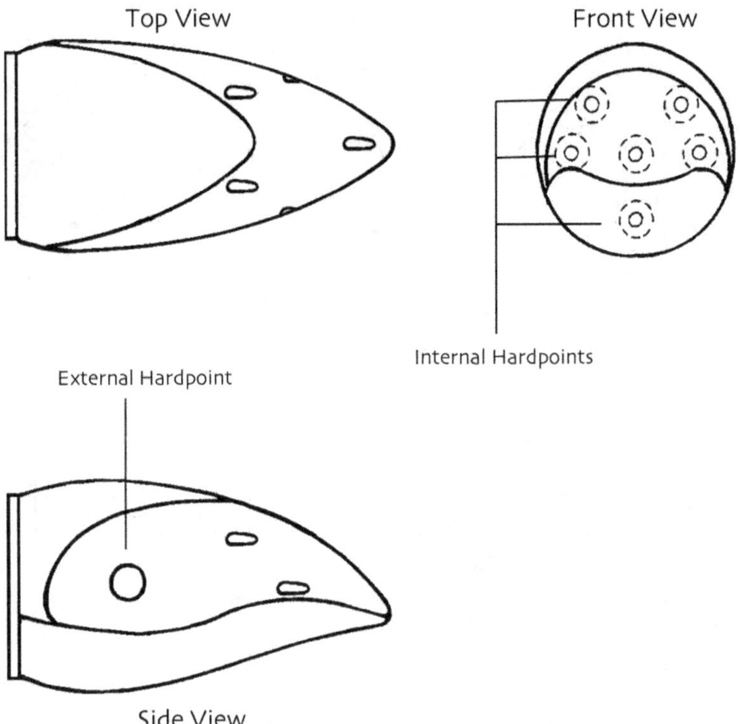

Spinner - Mk.III
Propulsion: Propeller

A spinner consists of two counter-rotating propellers. The original Mk.I had a total of 4 blades while the Mk.III has doubled that number to 8. The Mk.III spinner is capable of producing enough thrust to propel a single-seat fighter approximately 500 km/hr.

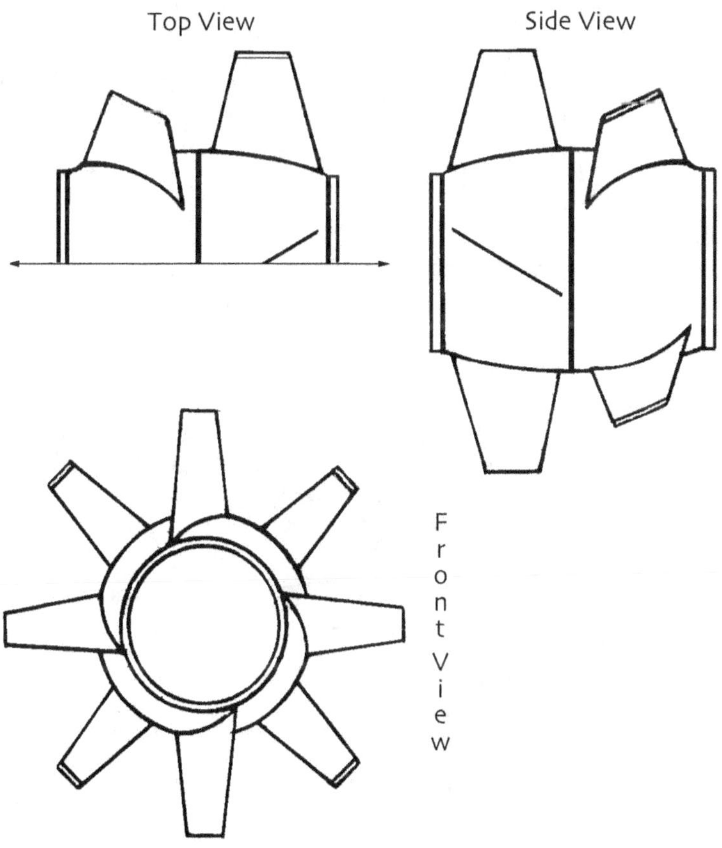

Spinner – Mk.V
Propulsion: Propeller

The Mk.V spinner is the 6-blade successor to the traditional pusher-prop design. It can provide enough thrust to achieve speeds up to 600 km/hr. Both the Mk.IV (5-blade) and Mk.V were outfitted with experimental blade shapes including: straight, bent-fin, and spiral-edge modifications.

Top View   Side View

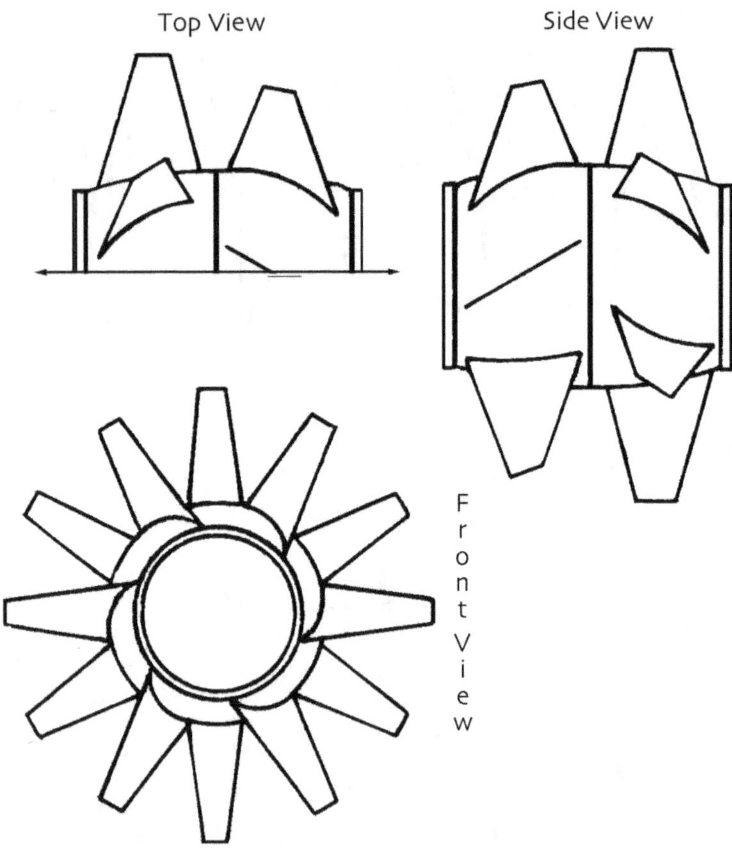

Stabilizer Mk.I

This variant of the main stabilizer is the standard airfoil utilized for fighter aircraft. Symetrical in design, it can be attached to a variety of external hardpoints. Early models were out fitted with a single 20mm canon, while subsequent versions added an additional 15mm canon.

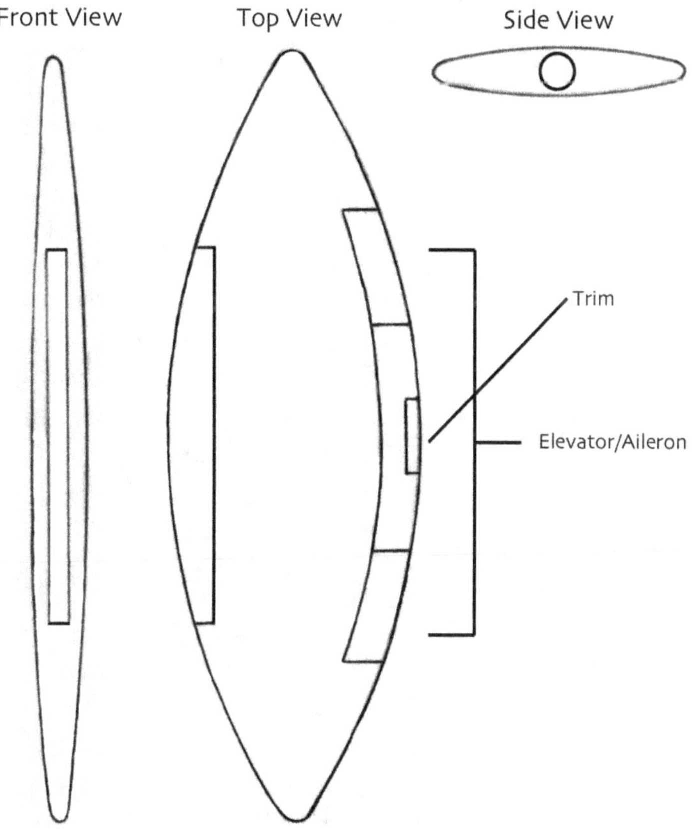

Stabilizer Mk. II

The Mk.II stabilizer was developed as a shorter
variant for use on intercept and reconnaissance
aircraft. At just over half the size of the standard
stabilizer, its smaller surface area allowed fan
powered wakemakers to increase speeds between
10-20% dependent on the configuration. Outfited
with a single 15mm cannon this version was often
mounted in an asymmetrical manner on
hard-docked fighters.

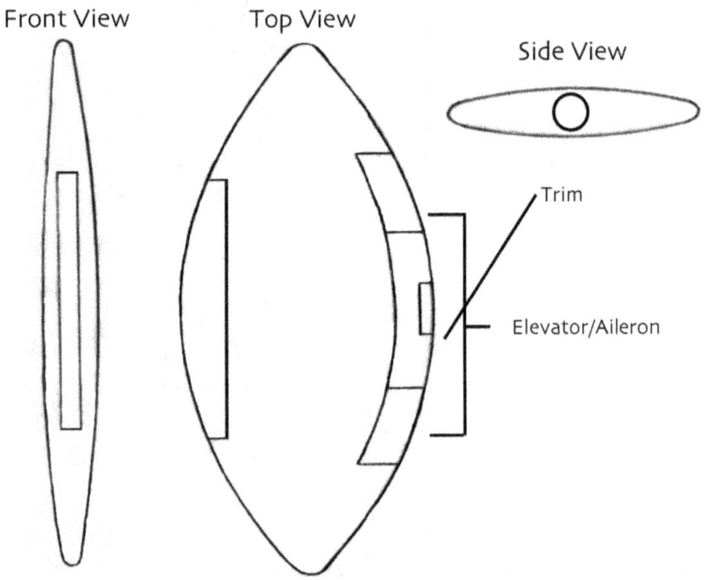

Stabilizer Mk.III

The Mk.III variant is the standard stabilizing airfoil for medium and heavy class bombers. Commonly referred to as the "shark fin," the Mk.III's sleek curves and asymmetrical design can support an external bomb load up to 500 kg. In addition, the Mk.III can also be converted for strike detail and fighter assignment with the addition of a 15mm or 20mm cannon. Fitted with two attachment hardpoints, the Mk.III can be "thin" mounted along its length for medium bombers or "wide" mounted along the end for heavy bombers.

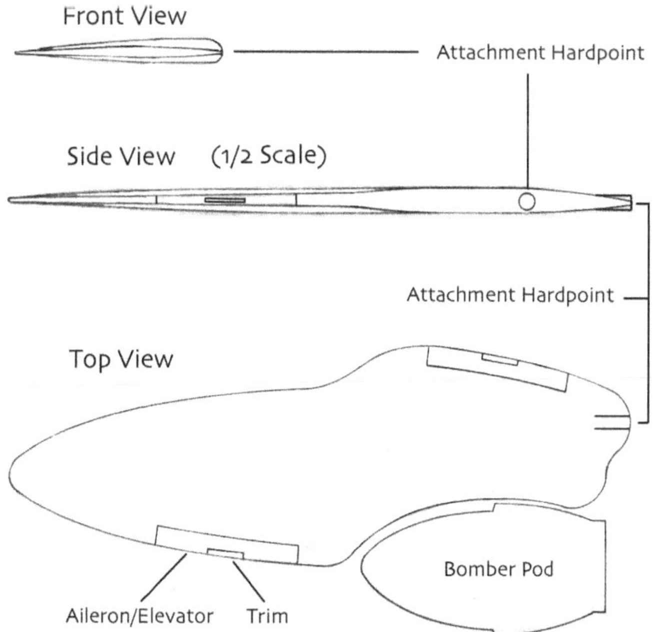

www.ingramcontent.com/pod-product-compliance
Lightning Source LLC
Chambersburg PA
CBHW070506300726
48975CB00007B/2348